The Coventry Gardens Serial Killer is John Nuzzolese's fourth novel. It promises to keep the reader in suspense from beginning to end.

When a cleverly disguised evil presence infiltrates Coventry Gardens, a British west coast township nestling within a stone's throw of Lands End, two New Scotland Yard detectives arrive on the scene to investigate a suspected serial killer's cryptic messages. According to Chief Inspector Matthew Ames this peculiar case resembled all the trappings of a copycat homicidal maniac who patterned his slayings after Agatha Christie's *Ten Little Indians* thriller.

The breathtaking climax of this spellbinding riddle takes place in the midst of an unforgettable intriguing set of circumstances. Superintendent Marshall Carter and a select few of his law enforcement sleuths design an amazing plan to include themselves as bargaining chips to comply with the demands of the deranged nemesis.

Kick off your shoes, sit back, relax, and enjoy the mystery.

WARNING: Do not take a sneak peek at the end of this novel. To savor the full enjoyment of this read- start from the beginning and proceed to its amazing climax. Respectfully, the author.

I0725596

ALSO BY JOHN NUZZOLESE

1. Devil's Cave The Treasure Lost: Circa 1600
2. Devil's Cave The Treasure Found: Circa 2000
3. Prince Louie, Catherine's Son:
   (Final episode of the Devil's Cave trilogy)
4. The Coventry Gardens Serial Killer

The Coventry Gardens
SERIAL KILLER

JOHN NUZZOLESE

Copyright © 2019 by John Nuzzolese.

ISBN Softcover   978-1-950580-18-7

All rights reserved. No part of this book may be reproduced or transmitted in any form or by any means, electronic or mechanical, including photocopying, recording, or by any information storage and retrieval system without express written permission from the author, except in the case of brief quotations embodied in critical reviews and certain other non-commercial uses permitted by copyright law.

Printed in the United States of America.

To order additional copies of this book, contact:
Bookwhip
1-855-339-3589
https://www.bookwhip.com

CONTENTS

DEDICATION

* * *

For the Father (Creator),

the Son, (Redeemer),

the Holy Spirit (Comforter) –

May those who have acknowledged and accepted the Three Divine Persons of the Blessed Trinity into their lives remain forever in God's presence.

PREFACE

It is difficult to discern the precise mechanism that triggers the mind of a serial killer into an explosive time bomb. We can never know the extent to which the mental state of an individual is affected at the time severe trauma, abuse, depravity, or an irrational dysfunction is experienced. In a manner of speaking, the abhorrence is manifested within the deepest recesses of the sub consciousness. At the precise moment of surrender, when the id submits itself to the dominant, primitive tendencies of evil, a terrible helplessness incenses one's thought processes to spontaneously yield to its hallucinatory cravings of inordinate impulses.

A healing agent for physical pain usually accomplishes what it is ordained to do. However, the human brain is composed of countless neurological nerve cells where insufferable disturbances remain dormant until at which time under severe pressure they surface and forcibly trigger unintelligible control of one's normal sensory perceptions. Successful treatment by a therapist for an existing mental problem, because of the mind's complexity, is often stymied by the patient's inability to contend with his or her personal disorientated malady.

How easy it is to prejudge anyone who has displayed injustice, betrayal, or even committed the most unimaginable crimes against us. Lest we forget, in the words of Jesus Christ when he said, "Love and forgive one another, as I have loved and forgiven you," is it not common sense for us to reason- being that we are all sinners, that we owe it to ourselves to indeed abhor the sin, but love the sinner?

God's *Love is patient, love is kind. It is not jealous, love is not pompous, it is not inflated, it is not rude, it does not seek its own interests, it is not quick-tempered, it does not brood over injury, and it does not rejoice over wrongdoing but rejoices with the truth. It bears all things, believes all things, hopes all things, endures all things.* [1 Corinthians 13:4-7]

If besieged by emotional or mental stress, it behooves mankind to leave these maladies *at the foot of the cross.* Our Lord and Savior Jesus Christ would sooner *behold His wounded sheep* surrendered to Him in trust.

MISSING PERSONS

In Order of their Disappearances

1. Peter Clayton   -   boarding house clerk
    Probable Cause of Death (shot in the temple?)

2. Jessica O'Brien   -   one room school teacher
    Probable Cause of Death (strychnine poisoning?)

3. Edgar Stevenson   -   part-time lighthouse keeper
    Probable Cause of Death (hanged by the neck?)

4. Simon McGivney   -   retired seaman
    Probable Cause of Death (shot through the skull?)

5. Dr. David Hardy   -   local physician
    Probable Cause of Death (dismemberment?)

6. Nathaniel Wingate   -   local parson
    Probable Cause of Death (drowned at sea?)

CHAPTER 1

Victim Number 4

As British Airways flight 117 approached Heathrow runway 27L for take-off, one of its passengers convulsed. Foam spewed profusely from his mouth causing hysteria throughout the second class cabin. Without delay the pilot taxied his craft back to its departure gate. Within an hour the jet, minus one voyager, lifted its wings and headed nonstop to New York. It was around this time a series of alleged slayings reportedly occurred in a coastal hamlet approximately 515 kilometers or 320 miles west of London.

About 1.25 miles off the coast of Lands End peninsula an indomitable mighty tower, Longships lighthouse, defies the sea. A protective barrier of rocks encircles its base. The lantern's automated light system (ten seconds bright ten seconds dark) and intermittent blasts of its fog horn warn seafarers when dense mist or rough sea storms engulf the point.

According to a cryptic note received by New Scotland Yard, sixty-five year old Simon McGivney, a retired experienced sailor, was maneuvering his sloop along the base of the unmanned tower when a bullet penetrated his skull. Chronologically he was number four in a series of three prior unconfirmed murders combing the vicinity of Coventry Gardens. Dr. David Hardy of the same quaint village nestling a few kilometers from the sea would likewise be identified in a third memo by the admission of a crazed lunatic as the fifth victim of a heinous spree of wanton slayings.

Ironically, London's prestigious detective bureau had not received any of these ghastly notifications until several weeks after they supposedly took place. It was then Chief Inspector Matthew Ames was summoned to Superintendent Marshall Carter's office. The feisty divisional commander of homicide spoke first.

"Matt, I hesitate to ask, being that your retirement from the force is. . ."

Ames interrupted, "Three weeks, two days, six hours," pausing to look at his watch, "and twelve minutes to be exact; boss, what can I do for you?"

"I wouldn't ask this, if it weren't absolutely necessary." Sympathetically, Carter added, "You see, Matt, I simply don't have anyone else to send."

"Send? Send where?" Whimsically, he injected, "Say no more. You want me to escort our beloved Queen Majesty on her forthcoming trip to New Zealand."

"I wish it were all that simple." Standing up, Superintendent Carter, heavyset in stature, ambled over to the huge map that covered practically the entire windowless wall adjacent to his desk. "Come," he motioned to Ames, "let's have a look."

Extremely curious, Matt approached the handsomely displayed projection of the British Isles and said, "What's up?"

Pointing to a sparsely populated area very close to the sea, Marshall said, "I'm sending you to Coventry Gardens to find out what the hell is going on over there. And take Constable Benjamin Steel with you."

"Who's he?"

"Oh, haven't you heard? The latest scuttlebutt has it he's the next boy wonder to Sherlock Holmes."

"Right! And I'm Watson."

"In any event your train leaves in an hour."

"Train, what, no wheels, chief?"

"You and your newly appointed partner will require time to put your noses to the grindstone and get acquainted with each other as well. Here, take this attaché case. On your way out Mahoney will give you a head's up on its contents. Constable Steel, by the way, whom I interviewed earlier, is the top rated graduate from this year's detective academy. Be nice to him."

"He's just a yearling!"

"Maybe so, but Ben is the best available man I've got right now." Carter added, "After reading the files I just gave you, perhaps you'll regret not retiring with Ryan Henson like everyone thought you would."

"And have my maximum pension plan downgraded, hell no? Besides, my ex-partner has a wife whose tearful supplications have indubitably rescued him from the subtle clutches of Scotland Yard."

Ignoring Ames's last comment Carter stood up and said, "Incidentally, Matt, the Coventry Gardens sheriff has been on leave for three weeks. He's due back today." With a brown leather carrier cuffed to his left wrist, Ames rose and vigorously shook Carter's hand. The veteran inspector then exited the superintendent's office. He hoped to God his new sidekick would be up to the task at hand.

C H A P T E R   2

The First Dossier

While the cross country express barreled its way toward Penzance, the last whistle stop for the Scotland Yard detectives, Inspector Ames reached for his satchel and retrieved the earliest dated dossier which alluded to the criminal death of Peter Clayton. A conspicuous number one had been stamped in red on the outer envelope. As it were, the elderly clerk, part-time lighthouse keeper, had been found dead in his bed. A bullet hole left blood oozing from his right temple.

Corresponding to the local physician's report, the murder must have taken place during the height of a thunderstorm that wreaked havoc in the area. No one heard the shot, and the poor bloke had been dead several hours before the body was discovered by a housekeeping employee.

Since no weapon was found at the crime scene, suicide had been ruled out. All else that could be discerned from the examiner's report, Clayton did not have any surviving relatives, and he spent most of his life in the military service before retiring to Coventry Gardens as a utility lighthouse keeper.

It didn't take long for the train's monotonous cadence to reel Constable Steel into a hypnotic state of oblivion. Amusingly, the lad's head bobbed rhythmically with the coach's constant sway of what seemed to be endless meandering tracks. Using his foot, Matt revived his newly appointed partner with a slight nudge. In reply Ben raised an eyebrow and said, "When do we eat?"

Curiously, Ames answered with, "Here, first earn your keep. Read this and tell me what you think." Handing the Clayton report to the rookie constable who had not fully awakened from his dreamy thoughts, Matt reached into his attaché case and removed the classified dossier with a large, red number two on its envelope.

CHAPTER 3

The Second Dossier

"With all due respect, sir, do you by any chance disapprove of having tea?"

"No, Constable Benjamin Steel, it's just that the dining coach will not be open for another half hour. Perhaps 'earn your keep' was a poor choice of words, but you and I must be on the same page before we reach our destination. It's my inherent duty to forewarn you we're on an extremely dangerous mission. Prior to our arrival at Coventry Gardens, it behooves us to learn each other's tactical approach of defense in the event we're confronted with a life threatening engagement. Our survival in this case may very well depend on anticipating one's partner's next move."

"Chief Inspector Ames, why exactly do you think I was selected for this particular assignment?"

"Perhaps Superintendent Carter saw something in you that hasn't yet crossed your mind. This I do know, constable, the boss believes and trusts in you, and that's good enough for me. However, try to remember, we're in this together. What I suggest is, from this moment forward, we prime ourselves for that which is to be least expected."

Steel nodded his head affirmatively. He then picked up the Clayton Report and without further ado began to read it carefully- as though his livelihood depended upon much more than a morsel of food. What Matt said was true. Ben understood from a briefing with Carter that he and his partner must work in tandem to uncover the identity of what might turn out to be a psychopathic serial killer who somehow lost all regard for human life.

Ames focused his attention on the second dossier. Jessica O'Brien, a seasoned school teacher, moved from Essex to Coventry Gardens to fill the vacancy at a local one room school house. It was a perfect haven for the fifty-two year old paraplegic. Aside from the peace and tranquility of the surrounding countryside and pristine shoreline, the rustic environment provided a suitable backdrop for writing her memoirs and poetry books, particularly during holiday breaks.

It had been indicated in Dr. Hardy's second dossier which was dated one day after Peter Clayton's reported death that Jessica had been poisoned with a lethal dose of strychnine, traces of which were found at the base of her tea cup. He also noted that Mrs. O'Brien's remains, he being her legal counsel, as prescribed in her last will and testament, be sent back to Essex and entombed with her husband who had passed away some time ago.

Dr. Hardy concluded his notation with: *A full report will follow. Good God! I've this very moment learned from an anonymous caller that Mr. Edgar Stevenson, one of our Viet Nam War heroes, was found dead in his cottage. Apparently the poor chap died of strangulation, so I have just been informed.*

CHAPTER 4

The Third Dossier

After Matthew Ames finished reading the second dossier, he looked up and noticed that Constable Steel was staring at him. Matt said, "So what did you think? No, don't answer that. We'll compare notes after tea. Here, read this one. It contains two mysterious deaths."

The younger detective quipped, "When I graduated from criminal division I hadn't imagined I'd be assigned to such an intriguing case as this, not my first time out."

Ames surveyed Steel and said, "Tell me about yourself. Since you and I will be working together, in addition to standard procedure, it's important we become well acquainted, a kind of getting to know one's partner sort of thing, to grasp a feeling for how he thinks."

The comely square-jawed junior detective said, "There's really not that much to tell. I'm twenty-seven years old, not married; and I was raised in Liverpool where I enjoyed playing cricket. Just before my sixteenth birthday a tragic event occurred that changed my life around."

"If it's not relevant, you don't have to discuss it."

"Inspector, it's what transpired that initiated my Scotland Yard career. I think you should know that my parents were among the fifty-two civilians killed in the London 05 metro terrorist bombings. Before Mum passed away she managed to eek out these last few words. *Benji,* she said, *Hal is gone.* He's my dad. *Don't mourn for us. Please son, make us proud by doing something good with your life.* At the same time I was always getting into all sorts of trouble. Other than what I just told you, that's basically my life's story in a nutshell."

"From where I'm sitting, you spoke volumes, constable." Pausing, Matt said, "As for me, I'm sixty-four and ready to retire. I've had two wives who both divorced me because I spent most of my evenings, like Superintendent Carter, at the office. It's just as well I don't have any children; I'd never have been able to spend much time with them anyway. Me, I'm a rugby fan," and with that he smiled and added, "I have a whole lot of interesting cases to bend your ear about, but right now we have to finish reading these dispatches. The dining car will be opening up in a few minutes."

After he read the first few lines of the third dossier, Ames's expression turned pensive. The memo arrived in London less than twenty-four hours following Hardy's second communiqué. He wondered how Constable Steel, whose youthful desire to make this world a better place in which to live, would perceive its contents. The missive read:

Superintendent Carter, at the moment I'm sitting at Dr. David Hardy's Computer. Of course, he doesn't really mind. The bare facts are I left Doc's entrails on his desk where I just now butchered him. Our personal war (yours and mine) will be over before you even realize it has begun. Oh yes. I think you should know that Simon McGivney's body by now has been washed out to sea. Who is Simon McGivney? You're the detective. Look for a corpse with a bullet hole in the center of its head. Toodle-oo.

When Constable Steel finished reading the second dossier, he looked up. This time Ames was staring at *him*. Matt said, "Read this. Then we'll eat; that is, if you still have an appetite."

CHAPTER 5

Tea

The express train's dining carriage was less than half full at the time Constable Steel and Chief Inspector Ames of Scotland Yard found a table where they would be least disturbed or overheard by other passengers.

In the process of checking out the menu Matt softly said, "Benjamin, you may order an alcoholic beverage if you wish. In all probability it will be the last one you'll be permitted to consume before we either solve the case or be replaced by higher authority."

"Or before we find ourselves in a meat grinder, strangled, or riddled full of bullet holes, partner."

Appreciating Steel's bit of dry humor, Matt said, "Those are definite possibilities that neither of us should forget to overlook."

A porter stopped by the table and said, "Which of you gentleman is Inspector Ames?"

Matt limply elevated his right hand and responded, "Guilty."

Handing Matt a sealed envelope, the courier said, "This message bearing your name was just forwarded to us from Scotland Yard. Ordinarily I would need to see some identification, but no sooner you looked up, I recognized your face, inspector."

Reaching into his pocket, Matt pulled out a quid and gave it to the kindly soft spoken porter.

"Thank you, sir. I've seen your photo in the London Chronicle many times. That's how I knew who you were. Good day," he said, and left.

After perusing the dispatch, Ames explained to Steel that Superintendent Carter made arrangements for them to stay at the Pendleton Hotel in Coventry Gardens, the same venue Peter Clayton, according to the first dossier, was found shot dead in his room. Upon disembarking from the train at Penzance, they would then gain access to a rent-a-car and proceed from there to their final destination where the heinous crimes allegedly took place. Carter included in the missive his usual admonition, *watch your backs, gentlemen.*

The dining car began to fill up quickly. Ames said, "We should be pulling into Penzance in little less than an hour. After we eat, we'll return to our compartment and discuss the best approach on how to proceed with what little information we have. Time is of the essence, so let's put it to good use."

Steel raised his champagne glass and said, "Ames, how is it that I never saw your photo in the newspaper?"

"Maybe you have. It may have been the time a reporter once took a picture of my derriere when I bent over to examine a piece of evidence; and you couldn't tell it was me." Holding up his drink Matt said, "Cheers!"

"Cheers!" Ben returned the salute.

And with that the two detectives swallowed their petite glasses of ginger ale in one fell swoop.

CHAPTER 6

Thinking Aloud

Constable Steel understood perfectly that once Ames and he returned to their compartment, everything from then on would be nothing but down to earth business. He was right. Matt retrieved two notepads from his case and said, "Ben," it was the first time he called him that, "I want you to review the documents you've just read and jot down anything that you would consider important, odd, or having any commonality that may appear to be linked to all three dossiers. Most likely our alleged serial killer took special precautions to cover his scent, but clever as he may be, in the process of repeatedly doing his dastardly deeds, he will invariably make mistakes that'll leave a paper trail pointing directly to him."

Looking at his watch Ames said, "We haven't much time. From Penzance we'll drive to Coventry Gardens. It shouldn't take more than forty-five minutes. In the meantime we'll examine the dossiers and crosscheck whatever elements are noteworthy. Perhaps during the course of our initial brain storming session something significant might surface that we can add to our investigative agenda."

The detectives completed their perusal of the documents simultaneously. Matt then proceeded to make a Venn diagram, two interlocking circles that indicated what each detective believed to be a point of significance in his investigation. Comparisons of the two lists bore interesting results. Ames penciled on the visual his and Steel's similarities and differences.

Pertaining to dossier #1, the two detectives agreed that it was odd Captain Peter Clayton's homicide was never reported to a local law enforcement agency at the time the corpse had been discovered. They also wondered what the term 'captain' denoted- 'sea captain' or 'captain of rank,' and could the killer have been someone the victim knew. Points that didn't match included: Matt wondered what became of Clayton's remains and Ben questioned if the killer might have been in the military service.

In regard to dossier #2, both Ames and Steel noted the following:

- Did Jessica poison herself, or did she die at the hands of an assassin?
- What caused Jessica O'Brien to become an invalid?
- Was Jessica a wounded war veteran?
- How long had she been teaching at Coventry Gardens?

Two differing points were: Ames considered whether O'Brien's memoirs or poetry books may possibly contain hidden clues as to who might have killed her; while Steel believed one of Jessica's neighbors may have recognized someone who had recently visited her home.

In reference to Edgar Stevenson, it would be interesting to know the method used that caused his strangulation, and if his being a Viet Nam War hero had to do with anything in particular.

Finally, dossier #3, Doc Hardy's cause of death, dismemberment, was a puzzlement, to say the least. Both Matt and Ben placed a question mark next to Hardy and McGivney's names. An extensive investigation had to be made before anything definitive could be formulated about either of them, or if indeed Dr. Hardy even wrote any of the cryptic messages.

Undoubtedly Superintendent Carter already commenced checking on wanted killers who employed the same wrinkle of behavior as documented in the dossiers. He had a network in his grasp that extended throughout every major communication center around the globe. In essence it would take a hell of a lot more than two field detectives lacking technical support to zero in on a crazed assassin. The perpetrator, who neglected to leave a calling card, was undeniably an incurable psychopath.

In a manner of speaking one detective was a seasoned agent and the other a greenhorn fresh out of the academy. Both Ames and Steel surmised that this particular criminal, daring to be caught, intended to play havoc with whoever picked up the gauntlet he had thrust at Scotland Yard. Simply speaking, aside from the alleged victims, the chief players in this case were a suspected lone serial killer and two commissioned law officers who had the entire network of Scotland Yard working on their behalf night and day.

Looking at Ben, Matt spoke words of encouragement, "I sense you're taking this assignment in stride. That's a good omen, constable. However, take nothing for granted. It's imperative we work together. Partners are dependent upon one another. Be ever vigilant, as I too must be, or else we'll both find ourselves, as the Yanks would say, *up shit's creek without a paddle.*"

CHAPTER 7

Coventry Gardens

Superintendent Carter at his word reserved a car at Penzance for the two detectives. The trip to Coventry Gardens took less than thirty-five minutes. Ames had made up his mind that he would not be intimidated by the serial killer's close proximity. Steel hadn't shown any signs of cowardice either. Matt liked him from the very start. He believed the young constable would make a fine inspector one day; that is, if he survived this particular bloody assignment.

Oddly enough, the quaint surroundings seemed to blatantly defy an evil presence. The air was so fresh, and the entire countryside reeked of a mixture of enchanting fragrances that captivated the senses. The locals carried on as though Ben and Matt ware typical tourists. By the looks of things no one seemed remotely concerned that some of the resident villagers had apparently been eradicated by a degenerate monster living in their midst.

Despite England's heavier than normal west coast tourist influx, Scotland Yard was able to procure a second floor suite for Ames and Steel. Upon their arrival at the Pendleton Hotel they needed to formulate an agenda, set up a direct communications center with London, and interview anyone who could shed light on the case, especially eyewitnesses or relatives and friends of the reportedly murdered victims. Both agents had to uphold the other in every circumstance, share their every thought, remain vigilant, and take nothing for granted. In essence they must concentrate wholeheartedly on piecing together all the missing elements of the extraordinary conundrum at hand.

After unpacking, and while Ben was washing up, Matt checked his email. Nothing from Carter. Matt raised his voice, "Hurry up in there, constable, we have a stop to make before we eat."

"Where to," Steel retorted?"

"The sheriff's office, he's got a lot of explaining to do."

"Ten-to-one," Ben shouted back, "he'll say he was out of town when all this kill, kill, kill crap was going on."

CHAPTER 8

Sheriff Rupert Hayes

Coventry Gardens law enforcement agency was within walking distance of the boarding house. Inspector Ames knew he needed to be in constant telephone contact with Superintendent Carter. He decided the logical place to set up headquarters would be at the local sheriff's office. Upon entering the establishment Matt said to the sheriff who was sitting at his desk, "I'm Chief Inspector Matthew Ames of Scotland Yard and this is my associate, Constable Benjamin Steel."

"Good evening, gentlemen, Sheriff Rupert Hayes at your service, what can I do for you?"

"We're here to verify the contents of certain letters that were forwarded to Superintendent Marshall Carter's office in a Dr. Hardy's name."

"Why don't you ask him yourself, his office is just down the road a piece? I don't mean to be abrupt, but I just now returned from being on holiday in the states, and I'm in the process of getting back into the sync of things."

"Told you so," whispered Ben under his breath.

Ignoring his partner's quip, Ames said, "According to the information Scotland Yard has obtained, at least five of your town's residents have been assassinated, including Dr. David Hardy from whose office the alert was given that these slayings in fact did occur."

"What? This is preposterous. When did all this happen? Who else was supposedly killed?"

"Apparently Superintendent Carter started receiving the cryptic letters just before you returned from your trip to the U.S., but the alleged murders, according to the dates on the actual typed memos, supposedly took place three weeks ago."

"You mean to say the post marks and times of the actual murders are not of the same accord?"

"That is correct, Sheriff. It's true we receive a number of erroneous dispatches whenever someone wants to grab a headline or two, but seldom do we receive any such as these."

Removing a paper from his attaché, Ames said, "To answer your question, Sheriff Hayes, here is a list of those reportedly killed. It's getting late. After you've had a chance to make some inquiries concerning the missing persons in question, Ben and I will meet with you tomorrow."

Somewhat perplexed the county officer affirmed, "I think that's a sensible approach. Do you have anything specific to do in the morning?"

"I believe Ben and I will make a routine surveillance, just to get acquainted with the area."

"Well then, come to my office at noon. We'll talk over lunch. Doc Hardy dead, I can't believe it. Be as it may, I want to welcome you both to Coventry Gardens. I'm sorry it couldn't have been under pleasanter circumstances, good day gentlemen."

No sooner the two detectives left the office, Matt spied an eatery. "What do you say we have a go at that bistro, Sherlock, and try to keep your mind off that nice skirt that just walked by? You and I have a big day ahead of us."

CHAPTER 9

Longships Lighthouse

After a good night's sleep, Ames and Steel made up an itinerary for the day. It appeared rather strange that the primly attired housekeeper, who served their morning meal, didn't utter an iota about anything unusual that may have transpired in the quaint Coventry Gardens village. However, she did insist upon two things.

"Gentlemen," she said, "*whatever you do, don't forget to have your pictures taken at the Lands End iconic signpost. The photographer will personalize it for you just as you say. And then you must try your luck on our tourist raffle tickets. The prizes are fabulous. Enjoy your visit. Now remember, this establishment does not serve noontime meals or supper. However, we do have the finest cuisine all up and down the strip. But of course you already know that- from the brochures. Until tomorrow, then, toodle-oo.*"

While driving to Lands End, Ames said, "Nice woman, we must remember to introduce ourselves tomorrow. I wonder how it is that she seems totally clueless as to what's been happening of late."

"The same notion occurred to me," Ben retaliated, "She seems the type who would bend your ear about nothing."

"Did you notice anything peculiar about Sheriff Hayes yesterday?"

"Only that he became suddenly flustered when he found out about what we knew and he didn't."

"That and something else," Matt noted.

"Like what, for instance?"

"His being absent precisely the length of time all the murders took place."

"I don't quite follow."

"Suppose Sheriff Hayes never went abroad. Suppose he was never on that flight across the pond. Did you ever think about that, constable?"

"Blimely," Steel quizzicaly said, "am I supposed to be thinking the way you do?"

Matt took Ben's last remark as a compliment. He said, "Let's do some moseying around before we rendezvous with the sheriff."

"Where're we going?"

"To scope out a lighthouse," Ames said.

"Which one, I can see three of them from here?"

"Longships, the albatross sticking up in the sky a mile off shore, that's where I think the weapon was used to kill Simon McGivney. According to the note in the third dossier, he was done away with before Dr. David Hardy had been supposedly butchered. The shooter had to be elevated above the victim for the missile to have entered the target at the trajectory it did. In any event, we'll first commandeer a boat at the wharf. You pilot."

"Okey-dokey."

Ames and Steel pulled up to the boat harbor at Lands End. Producing their credentials to the marine officer in charge, they requisitioned a small craft and motored out to the lighthouse. After mooring the vessel at Carn Bras, the largest rock upon which the beacon was erected, the two investigators proceeded to climb the exterior tower's vertical ladder.

Aside from the breathtaking view, a spray of mist blanketed the shoal where incoming waves pummeled the base of the cylindrically shaped obelisk. A sudden rush of euphoria captivated the two city detectives. They had momentarily been caught up in a capsule of awe inspiring exhilaration, the likes of which neither of them had ever experienced. It was though Matt and Ben were preyed upon by nature's inexplicable wonderment.

The ricochet of a single bullet striking within a few inches of Matt's head jolted both men from their stupor. In a flash they scampered down the lighthouse steps. Whether the missile had been intended to purposely kill or serve as a forewarning, Ames could not be sure. The shooter certainly had the two Scotland Yard officers at his mercy.

When the detectives were making their way back to shore Matt said, "In all probability McGivney was not shot from the tower. The report must have originated somewhere along the cliffs. His sniper must have felt safer there and he had to have used a long range rifle to boot. Ben, let's not mention anything about this to Sheriff Hayes. From the little we know of the bloke I don't think he's in a position to help us any more than we can explain to him why anyone might want to take a pop shot at us. The way it was cited in the last communiqué McGivney was indeed victim number four."

"Yeah, and Doc's number five, and you and me numbers six and seven," Steel blurted out.

Wincing at his partner's remark Matt said, "Ben, when we were scurrying for our lives at the time of the gun shot, did you recall inhaling a foul odor, something rancid perhaps?"

"Come to think of it, I did. It may have been the smell of dead fish or someone's garbage washing up against the rocks."

"Or rotting seaweed perhaps," Ames added, "Or maybe even something else."

CHAPTER 10

Sheriff Hayes's Report

An appetizing lunch arrived at the same time Ames and Steel entered Sheriff Rupert Hayes's office at twelve noon sharp. He greeted the Scotland Yard ambassadors with a smile and said, "The specialty of the day is Cornwall's finest pasties filled with steak, onions, and potatoes. On the sweet side there's jam filled pasties with apples, plums, strawberries, you name it."

Turning to the delivery boys, Rupert said, "Thank you gentlemen, my sincerest compliments to the chef." The couriers left as Hayes remarked to his honored guests, "Terry's Restaurant, which providentially happens to be next door, has the finest cuisine in all southwest England. Shall we eat first and talk later, or talk as we eat?"

Steel chimed in, "I'll just help myself while you two talk, if that's okay with you guys."

Ames shot back, "Constable Steel, if it's all the same with you, I believe it will be expedient for us all that we eat at the same time." Would you like to say grace, sheriff, or shall I?"

The meal was as Hayes said it would be, simply delicious. When it appeared everyone was satisfied with sufficient food and drink, Matt reached for his attaché case. Ames said in a tone that was not indicative of his usual manner, "Folks, what do you say we get down to business? Rupert, supposing we begin with you. Could you tell us what it is you found out so far?" Steel readied himself to take notes.

Not knowing exactly how to begin what he actually wanted to say, Hayes shifted in his chair and spoke in a solemn voice, "Gentlemen, frankly, as difficult it is for me to say, I made several inquiries and came up with only this. A handful of our Coventry Gardens citizens have mysteriously made traveling plans without informing their neighbors."

CHAPTER 11

Rupert's Revelations

Sheriff Hayes clasped his hands and proceeded to give this report. "Astonishing it may seem, this is what I know. The disappearances reportedly began shortly after I left Coventry Gardens for London's Heathrow Airport twenty three days ago."

Rupert paused for a moment and then continued with, "In the case of Doc Hardy, at first I surmised he may have been called out of town on an emergency summons. That didn't happen. If he had, in my absence, David would have first notified Parson Nathaniel Wingate. His vicarage is just across Turnbull Lane from where Doc resides. Come to think of it, when I tried to confer with the parson, he wasn't at home. Perhaps *he* knows something. I then checked with Doc's neighbors and regular clients. The last anyone had seen of him was three weeks ago. It was assumed Hardy went somewhere on a holiday. After our conference here is completed, we'll go to his place and have a look around."

Steel was scribbling down notes as fast as he could. "Next," Hayes rambled on, "I learned there has been a few inquiries by some of our citizens concerning Jessica O'Brien, a sweetheart of a teacher. The school is on Spring break, but a neighbor, Harriet Jones, calls on her every day to see if she was in need of anything. O'Brien is an invalid. It's doubtful she would have left town without first informing anyone. Ms. Jones has a passkey to her cottage. She used it several times to see if Jessica perhaps returned from visiting with a friend, but everything seemed to be in order- other than Mrs. O'Brien not being there."

Rupert paused, "Am I going too fast for you, constable?" Steel shook his head from left to right. Hayes continued his chatter, "I even took a quick look around myself. Nothing appeared suspicious that would make one wonder that something was amiss. Oh yes, three weeks ago Harriet informed a neighbor, Hiroki Takahashi, he's Japanese, of Jessica's mysterious absence. He made it known at the shire's office (that anyone who had information of the schoolmarm's whereabouts) to give Harriet a buzz. Thus far she's heard nothing."

Ben was up to his eyeballs in taking notes. He already broke one pencil point. "Thirdly," Sheriff Hayes pressed forward, "we have a few recluses in Coventry Gardens that haven't been seen by anyone during the time period of my absence, but that doesn't necessarily imply that they're missing. After we're finished at Doc's place, I'll follow up with these other three."

Ames asked, "What other three?"

"The recluses I mentioned a moment ago."

"Can you tell me their names?"

"Of course I can tell you their names. I'm the sheriff, ain't I? It's my business to know everyone's name around here."

Steel chocked, but did not look up. He could hardly contain himself. It was then he broke his second pencil point.

"That you are," Ames answered Haye's redundant question. "May I please have the names of the personages you just now alluded to, for the record?"

"Certainly. Peter Clayton, Edgar Stevenson, and Simon McGivney, that's capital M lower case c, then capital G lower case i v n e y. Frankly, I don't know too much about any of them, but I have the means of working up a profile on any of our residents."

"Thanks, sheriff, I'll just leave this packet for you to peruse at your earliest convenience. I'm confident you'll find the contents most interesting. After you've read everything, I believe we'll all be on the same page. Right now I think it's about time we check out Doc

Hardy's place. Incidentally, if it's okay with you, Ben and I will set up a communications center right here in your headquarters- to keep in constant touch with our superiors."

"Be my guest. I have a spare room down the hall you can use. It even has a trunk line to London."

"Splendid. With that being settled Constable Steel and I thank you for a most scrumptious lunch. What do you say we inspect Doc's residence?"

"You are indeed quite welcome, inspector. And now, if you'll kindly follow me, gentlemen, we'll be on our way. I'll say this much; if anyone has messed with any of our Coventry Gardens citizens, whoever is responsible will wish he'd never been born."

CHAPTER 12

Parson Wingate

Ames and Steel accompanied Sheriff Hayes to David Hardy's residence. A grand view of the sea could be seen from the terrace. Distant waves spewed clusters of white foam along the southern shores of the peninsula. It was not necessary for Rupert to use forced entry. The front door had been opened by Parson Wingate who possessed a passkey to the physician's quaint red brick cottage. Ames noticed what seemed to be a rather large dust cloth in Nathaniel's hand.

"Oh, hello sheriff," the clergyman spoke first, "I'm just doing a little tidying up for Doc Hardy. He asked me to look after things until he returns."

"Return from where," Ames asked?

"Who might you be?" The parson's voice probed curiously.

It was then Sheriff Hayes injected, "Pardon for the interruption, Nathaniel, I would like for you to meet Chief Inspector Ames and Constable Steel from Scotland Yard. They're looking for the whereabouts of a few missing persons. Doc Hardy happens to be one of them. Parson, could you please tell us when exactly did you last see him?"

"Let's see, about three weeks ago David Hardy left a key in my letter box with a note indicating that it was necessary for him to leave town on personal business, and that he wanted me to monitor his residence until the doc returned. I thought I'd tidy up a bit as well."

Ames said, "Nathaniel, do you still have the message in your possession?"

"I believe so, stop by the personage any time tomorrow. I'll have it for you then. However, if you will all excuse me, at the moment I have an important engagement with one of my parishioners and a council meeting after that. In whatever else I can be of service, I will be more than happy to assist you. Good day, gentlemen."

Dr. Hardy's place was given a thorough investigative walk-through. Nothing appeared to be disturbed. There certainly hadn't been any signs of entrails. However, the possibility existed that if the innards were gutted out in the physician's office, someone was very meticulous in cleaning up the mess afterward.

Upon checking for messages at the boarding house, Ames and Steel returned to the sheriff's office to set up a command post with Scotland Yard. It didn't take very long for Hayes to change his tune after reading the dossiers Matt had left on his desk.

"Whoever this bloke is, he's a nut job, an animal of the worst kind. Inspector Ames, surely you must have *some* clout. We need an *army* down here!"

CHAPTER 13

Benjamin's Dilemma

The next morning, Ames asked the cheerful breakfast server her name. In the stout woman's usual bubbly manner she said, "I'm Mrs. Melanie Belldonger. When you hear the steeple bell ringing, you think for me," and she giggled.

"Ames smiled and said, "I've been meaning to ask you, whatever became of Mr. Clayton?"

"You mean Peter Clayton?"

"Yes, that's the chap."

"It's a strange thing, if I'm permitted to say, but Mr. Clayton, God bless his soul, a finer gentleman you would ever want to meet; he used to be the senior clerk of this very establishment. Wouldn't you know the bloke up and left without saying anything to anyone? The proprietor, Mr. Cyrus Pendleton, made inquiries as to Mr. Clayton's present situation, but no one's seen 'im for three weeks."

Ames explained that he and Steel were Scotland Yard detectives on holiday, and should Melanie ever have the slightest reason to call upon them for anything, they lived just upstairs. The Chief Inspector's remarks exhibited a grin on Mrs. Belldonger's broad, chubby cheeks.

Eager to compliment the housemaid, Steel said, "Melanie, Matt and I are extremely impressed by your extraordinary warmth and grace."

"Why thank you, I'm overwhelmed; such fine gents you are, and I mean that sincerely."

The breakfast nanny then leaned over the table and said in a soft voice, "It's true my memory isn't what it used to be, but no matter, through the years I've kept the good and the bad in my journal. For the times folks have been kind to me or pretended to be kind; it's all there in black and white."

And with that, "If there's nothing else I can get you boys, you'll have to excuse me. I need to take a tray over to Parson Wingate. While making a cup of tea last night he burned his hand on the stove. The vicar's such a credit to our community. We're so fortunate to have him; till tomorrow, toodle-oo!"

After she left, Ben looked at Matt and said, "I wonder what she meant by all that good and bad, black and white gibberish."

Matt replied with an air of indifference, "Beats me."

Changing the subject Steel said, "Partner, I was thinking."

"Nothing wrong with that," Ames quipped."

"Seriously, something doesn't add up."

"What's niggling at you, constable?"

"I'm a little confused as to who's been sending all the dossiers. Both McGivney and Hardy were supposedly eliminated according to the third communiqué."

"Oh that, it's really quite simple. In all probability the delusional serial killer, if indeed he truly exists, is obviously attempting to create a reenactment of the *Ten Little Indians* ploy, which is solely intended to muddle Scotland Yard."

"Say, what?"

"I'll explain it all to you during our 'think' walk."

CHAPTER 14

Ten Little Indians

Matt reviewed the day's agenda to his partner. He said to Ben, "Constable, we need to stop at the vicarage, discuss a few things with Superintendent Carter, see what the sheriff has come up with, and take a ride to Lands End- though not necessarily in that order."

"You must enjoy being shot at."

"No, what you intimate is true. It does behoove us both to stay clear of the lighthouse. However, the ocean air is inebriating, don't you think?"

Steel answered facetiously, "Sure, after having a few gin and tonics."

While the two detectives walked along the shoreline, Matt said, "Keep your eyes peeled for lofty places where a sniper has the advantage of taking a clear shot at us."

"Yes, sir, they're already peeled, like an orange."

"Good, do you recall what our phantom murderer said in the note that accompanied the third dossier, that he had already killed Simon McGivney before performing inside-out surgery on Hardy?"

"How can I not remember?"

"Well, McGivney reminds me of the fourth victim in Agatha Christie's novel, *Ten Little Indians*. The sequence of events had an unusual twist. You must have read it before graduating from school."

"Can't say I have, perhaps I was distracted by more important things at the time it came out."

"In your dreams, you weren't even born when the book was published; I believe sometime in the mid-sixties."

Matt suddenly paused in his stride.

"What is it?" Ben inquired.

"Sorry, it's just that I saw something. It was only a gull perched on a roof."

"Your suggestion that one of us walks backward while the other faces the opposite direction was very astute."

"It's called *watch your partner's* back."

"The *Ten Little Indians* twist, what about it?"

"Ben, the story is a masterpiece. I really don't want to spoil it for you."

"I insist. Spoil it for me. What's the connection?"

"Okay, we need to discuss it anyway. You see there were a string of murders in an old mansion on this deserted island. The assassin, who planned the whole thing, included himself among eight guests and two servants that received an invitation to attend this gathering. The perpetrator erroneously believed everyone at the assemblage was responsible for committing wrongful deaths and endeavored to even the score.

"As it turned out, the party goers soon realized they were being bumped off one by one, and there was no way of getting off the island. This case appears to have an uncanny resemblance of the *Ten Little Indians* nursery rhyme, from which Agatha Christie patterned her book. You see, Ben, there is a distinct possibility our suspected serial killer adopted the identical blueprint for murder that Christie's assailant used. But there's no way of knowing, because we haven't uncovered a dead body yet."

Ames paused again. He proceeded to say, "This is what I've been leading up to; the *Ten Little Indians* murderer, a retired judge, conspired with one of the guests, a physician, to pretend to shoot 'his honor' using blanks when no one else was in the room. After everyone who heard the shot came running to the scene where the corpse lay on the floor with red dye oozing from his chest, the doctor- who hid himself behind the door, rushed up to the body, pretended to examine it, and pronounced the imposter dead. The purpose for this charade was to enable the victim to secretly spy on the others in hopes of flushing out the real killer. Naturally the physician was the next one to die, because now the real murderer, the judge, could never be suspected- since he was supposedly already dead."

"Matt, hold on for a sec." Steel's voice generated excitement. "How many people were killed in the story before the bogus murder took place?"

"Three were killed, and the fourth victim was the dummy corpse."

"Of course, then it must follow, If we're dealing with a copycat murderer…" Ben thought for a moment, "*Simon McGivney* was victim number *four*. He must be the Coventry Gardens Serial Killer! Of course, *Doc* was number *five*. Yep, Simon McGivney's our man."

"Brilliant deduction, Watson, not so fast; remember- as I said before, murders = corpses. We haven't found any yet."

"How do you account for the lighthouse incident yesterday?"

"It tells me someone is openly challenging Scotland Yard to seek him out, and yet the crazed lunatic doesn't want the curtain to come down until his killing spree has been satisfied- if indeed our alleged assassin has actually killed anyone."

On the way back to the sheriff's office Ben said, "Matt have you noticed anything?"

"Such as, constable?"

"Since we've appeared on the scene, no one else has been reported missing."

"Don't hold your breath, detective, we've been here less than two days and, as you well know, already taken for a couple of clay pigeons."

CHAPTER 15

A Sixth Victim

mes and Steel noticed the sheriff's car speeding in the opposite direction on their return to town.

"It's a good thing you asked him for a key to his office," Steel said. "The poor guy must be at his wits end. I wouldn't want to be in his shoes."

"He seems to be bearing up to the situation. When you think of it the man has no choice. Let's check in with Superintendent Carter before we keep our appointment with the parson."

The phone in Ames and Steel's makeshift office was ringing when they arrived.

"Ames speaking."

"Matt, It's Carter. Are you sure this is a private line?"

"Not to worry, we've fixed it where Sheriff Hayes can't listen in on us, even if he wanted to."

"Good, hold on to your hat. I just now received an email originating from the Penzance Library from Dr. David Hardy. I thought he was dead. It makes me sick to repeat it."

"Be sick, Repeat it."

"Okay, after I read it, I'll forward you a hard copy. It says:

Superintendent Carter, the two infantrymen you sent to Coventry Gardens are clueless. From under their very noses I've sent Parson Nathaniel Wingate to his Maker. He knew too much. Inform your plebs they can find him in his vicarage with a crucifix stuffed down his throat. Recall your troops. I could have killed your two scouts yesterday. Beware; their turn to die is fast approaching, and I might add; so is yours. Dr. Hardy

"Matt, what the hell was he referring to 'could have killed you and Steel yesterday' 'Beware; their turn to die' and now it's mine as well? I need to know what's going on down there."

"It's all in my report, Marshall, I'll email everything to you after Ben and I check on Wingate. Try not to worry about us. We can take care of ourselves. When the first corpse turns up, that'll confirm our serial killer is playing for real. In the meantime, have the weapons division forward me a list of sniper rifles that have an accuracy range of a mile and a half. And, by the way, Marshall, we both know that it doesn't amount to a hill of beans whose name is signed to a slew of 'Looney Tunes' dispatches. For all we know the Prime Minister's mistress is behind this whole thing."

"Be careful of what you say, Matt. Another crack like that will cost you- big time." Click.

After Ames hung up, Steel said, "What was that all about?"

"Ben, I'm afraid you spoke too soon. Carter received another poison pen letter from Dr. Hardy."

"I thought he was dead."

"That's what Marshall just said. Apparently Parson Wingate, the sixth little Indian, has allegedly met his Maker. According to what Carter was led to believe, if it's not another phony story, we should find him in the vicarage with a crucifix stuffed down his throat."

CHAPTER 16

Mrs. Belldonger's Concern

Mrs. Belldonger was coming down the steps of the vicarage when the two detectives happened to be going up. "Good morning gentlemen, you don't by any chance know where I can find Parson Wingate? I left this breakfast tray in the foyer over an hour ago, as I usually do whenever he rings over for one, but he hasn't touched it."

Ames said, "Constable Steel and I had planned on conversing with Nathaniel today and thought this would be a convenient time to see him. Is it possible for him to have overslept this morning?"

"When I knocked on the parson's door and called out to him, there was no answer. I took it upon myself to gain entrance the usual way but had no success."

"Which way is that?" Steel injected.

"By turning the doorknob," she said quite sincerely. "And no, inspector, I've never known Nathaniel to oversleep."

"Mrs. Belldonger," Matt asked, "who else might possess a key to the parson's residence?"

"I believe Shire Latham has a key to the vicarage. To my understanding the premises belongs to the municipality."

"Thank you Mrs. Belldonger, Constable Steel will take that tray over to the boarding house for you." Turning to Ben he said, "I'll procure a key from the local administrator and then meet you back here in twenty minutes. Watch your back."

As he turned to leave, Ames could hear Mrs. Belldonger ask Ben, "What did Inspector Ames mean when he said, *watch your back?*"

The cordial shire, Mr. Reed Latham, was very cooperative with Ames; that is, after he showed the country executive positive ID. The magistrate mentioned nothing about the missing persons; so Matt thought it best to refrain from speaking about them for the time being. Reed said, "Give my regards to the good parson. You can leave the key with him, or hold on to it if you need to check back with him later."

By the time Ames returned to the vicarage he noticed Steel patiently sitting on the steps. Ben told him Mrs. Belldonger was a bit concerned with Wingate's not responding to her call, and could she please be kept informed, if they learned anything.

The two entered the parson's residence and called out to him. Being there was no answer, they inspected the premises. Finding nothing that would raise an eyebrow, for the exception of a disconnected answering machine, Matt's tone of voice denoted his frustration. "No parson, no note; the place is immaculate. We'll inform the Yard there's a distinct possibility that we may have another missing person on our hands. What do you say we reanalyze the cryptic messages we received from our alleged phantom friend? Who knows, perhaps an obscure clue we may have missed earlier will jump out at us."

"Hope you're right, partner, it's about time we *copped* a break. No pun intended."

CHAPTER 17

A Talk with Carter

Today lunch had to be placed on the back burner. Matt and Ben's plates were filled with more immediate concerns. After returning from Parson Wingate's cottage, Ames had Carter on the phone.

"What did you find out, Matt?" the superintendent asked.

"No sign of Parson Wingate. Ben and I searched his residence thoroughly."

Carter said, "The Home Secretary in charge of military records found a common factor that profiles all the missing persons as having been enlisted in some branch of the British armed forces. We'll keep you posted, if there's anything more to it. So far, Parson Nathaniel Wingate, whoever this bloke is, draws a blank. He could be using an alias. I'll fax everything to you shortly. See what you and Steel can make of it."

"Thanks, Marshall, Ben and I will be scrutinizing the last two communiqués you received from our phantom friend. We talked it over and are convinced all the earlier dossiers were designed to lead us astray."

"What you said makes perfect sense; Matt, there's one more thing."

"Shoot."

"I'm sending a low reconnaissance flier to take photos of the entire area, to see if there're any signs of discoloration where the earth may have been disturbed. Maybe we can get lucky and find a few mounds of recently plowed up soil. The missing dead bodies have to be buried somewhere. Watch your back, and tell your sidekick to do the same. Talk to you later."

Turning to Steel, Ames said, "Constable, let's get cracking, it's time I've earned *my* keep."

CHAPTER 18

A Headless Corpse

Scotland Yard confirmed that none of the missing persons belonged to the same military unit or were closely associated to one another prior to taking up residence in the Coventry Gardens community. The two dossiers in which the self-proclaimed killer made reference to himself were scrutinized. However, after Ben carefully studied the documents, Matt pointed to an interesting word on the third dossier that had aroused his attention. He said, "Ring a bell, as in Belldonger?"

"*Toodle-oo!* Of course," Steel exclaimed, "How could I have missed it?"

"Don't get down on yourself, Ben. It may not even be important. We'll look into it later. Right now I want to explore something this bloke alluded to in his last two transcripts. They captivate my interest. In the one he talks about this entire charade as being part of a war; and in the other, he's making you and me out to be infantrymen. Our suspect could be an ex-soldier, or perhaps has a vendetta against anyone wearing a uniform."

"Maybe he has a bone to pick with Scotland Yard as well," Ben asserted.

"Perhaps, but I can't help keep from thinking this poor soul must have gone off the deep end. Something tells me there's a bunch of bodies stowed away somewhere and he wants us to find them."

"Why?"

"So he can kill us both at the precise time we locate his crypt of souvenirs. He also has a vendetta for Carter. As I see it the psychopath is convinced he's in control and can pick the time and place for whomever he chooses to liquidate."

"You're beginning to scare me, partner."

"If it's true that we're currently in the midst of a reenactment of Christi's *Ten Little Indians* scenario, the murderer must still eliminate four more people before his spree is over. However, in regard to our case, I don't believe the killer intends to do away with himself, as he did in Agatha's novel. Perhaps he's not even concerned with counting dead bodies."

"Then how is Christi's *Ten Little Indians* and the Coventry Gardens conundrum alike?"

"Perhaps they're coincidental. It's quite possible our clever alleged assailant never read the novel. If I'm guessing correctly, when he's finished his ghastly business here, he'll most likely move on to some other place and start all over again until he's either caught or killed."

"So then why does he have his meat hooks out for us, and who do you think is behind all this?"

"It could be any of the victims, or maybe someone just pretending to be a happy-go-lucky country bumpkin, like Mrs. Belldonger. Ben, this entire thing started three weeks before we arrived. Tourists come and go every day. It's mind boggling. No one has the faintest clue that anything unusual is going on around here, excepting for Scotland Yard, Rupert, and our nemesis.

"To answer your first question, the crippled mind of this particular serial killer has appointed himself alien general and we're the enemy foot soldiers. Whoever is behind all this has obviously contracted an emotional disorder or mental disturbance that's taken complete control of his faculties. I suspect Carter feels the same way. I've never known him to burn the midnight oil on any case, as he's been doing with this one."

It was just then Sheriff Hayes entered his office. "Gentlemen," he raised his voice loud enough to be clearly heard, "do you have a moment, I have some rather heart-rending news to share with you?"

Ames said, "Rupert, you look like you've just seen a ghost?"

"I wish I had. This morning Harbor Patrol retrieved a body along the shores of Lands End, in the vicinity of Longships lighthouse. I've been there all day interviewing anyone who may have seen something. Sadly to say the corpse had somehow been decapitated, however the torso was still intact. It could be Parson Wingate. The victim was wearing a rabat. Nathaniel may have been fishing late last night, as often is his practice."

Ames turned to Ben and said, "Call Carter. Tell him what's happened. Let's go, sheriff. I'd like to see the scene where the body was found."

As Matt and Rupert were leaving the office, Steel yelled over to Matt, "Try not to take too long. I'm kind of looking forward to enjoying our last meal together."

Hayes looked at Ames and said, "What did he mean by that?"

Closing the door behind him Matt answered with, "I haven't the foggiest idea. All I know is he likes to eat."

/ CHAPTER 19

Ripple of Shock

mes and Sheriff Hayes viewed the cadaver. Matt said, "The body may have been catapulted into the water by a deep sea swell. Its head then could have gotten caught up in the craft's motor shaft, or perhaps the jaws of a rogue shark. Either of the two possibilities would explain the jagged edges along the neck-line of the deceased. However, it will take a forensic pathologist to determine the exact cause of what really happened."

A queasy feeling enveloped Ames when he looked up and glanced toward Longships lighthouse. It seemed to be beckoning to him in an ominous voice; *Go home. Your hour is nigh. Take Constable Benjamin Steel with you. Don't be a fool. Go home.* Turning his head away Matt indicated with a nod to the marine officer in charge that he was through and the remains should be transported to the morgue.

"Inspector," Sheriff Hayes's voice sounded dispirited, "if there's nothing else; I'll drop you off at the office and then inform Latham of what occurred here. The shire's not going to like it; tourist season you know."

Matt reached into his pocket and retrieved a solitary key. "Take this," he said, "Give it to Reed. Tell him I won't be needing it anymore."

"I've been meaning to say, Ames, from here on in we share and share alike."

"You must be referring to the incident where Ben and I nearly bought it at the lighthouse. How'd you find out about that?"

"It's my business to know, and if it so happens that the corpse just hauled out of here belongs to Parson Nathaniel Wingate, whoever it was that wanted his head for a trophy, his ass is grass, and I'm the lawnmower."

Ames, having duly noted Sheriff Rupert Hayes's pronounced New York witticism, mumbled under his breath, *Yanks.*

CHAPTER 20

AWSM

"How did it go?" Ben greeted Ames. "From the grim expression on your face the news isn't all that good."

"The unidentifiable body's cause of death is yet to be determined, aside from the fact the cadaver in question is minus one head. It's too soon to tell if the victim is Parson Wingate, however a rabat was tied to his waist."

"What's a rabat?"

"It's a clergyman's black shirt front which signifies he's a man of the cloth. I'd better inform Carter."

"Marshall's waiting for your call now. He also forwarded the information you requested on the AWSM. The photos are awesome."

"Carter can wait; let's have a look. It had to be an AWSM the sniper used to zero in on us at the lighthouse. There must be one around here somewhere."

The AWSM (Arctic Warfare Super Magnum) rifle has a maximum range of 8,120 feet (1.54 miles or 2.47 kilometers.) Pictures of the high tech rifle forwarded by Carter were accompanied by a video which had been produced by the U.S Department of Defense and employed by British Intelligence in their munitions training program.

Matt soon found what he'd been looking for. The British adopted the long range bolt-action sniper rifle with its high powered telescopic sight while engaging its troops in the Afghanistan and Iraq confrontations.

Ames said, "Let's see if any of our missing persons had been trained to use a high powered weapon."

Forty-five minutes of checking and crosschecking yielded nothing. Ames said, "This is getting us nowhere. There just aren't any listings available for us to ascertain the specific information we're looking for."

"Matt, it was well worth the try; is there anything we've overlooked, anything at all?"

"I was just thinking. If Parson Wingate and the headless corpse are one and the same, it stands to reason the padre may have witnessed something, and the serial killer needed to remove him from his bucket list."

"That's true, Matt, but if the dead person isn't Wingate- we're back to square one."

It was then Sheriff Hayes entered the office. Rupert looked rather perturbed. "Gentlemen," he said, "I had a long discussion with Reed Latham. I explained what occurred, and he insisted we do not postpone the pre-arranged meeting in the town center scheduled in a couple of days, Thursday, I believe."

Matt responded, "You mean to say the shire isn't going to alert the public of a possible malevolent presence?"

"Correct, he intends to push forward in launching this year's tourist season as scheduled. Evidently five missing persons and one accidental death, no matter who it is, should not be sufficient reason to cause needless panic."

Ben shook his head in dismay. He said, "Any confirmation on what may have killed the man found dead in the sea?"

"Too soon to tell, however, our mortician Larry Quinton is looking into the matter."

"I should hope so." Realizing that what he just said could be construed to mean something else, Steel said, "Well, you know what I mean."

Ames needed to do a little probing. "Sheriff, would you happen to know anyone that might possess a high powered rifle?"

"Simon McGivney had one. I know because he let me use it to take a couple of shots at a marker north of Longships lighthouse; I missed both times, at least his binoculars indicated I had."

Steel looked at Ames. They were both thinking the same thing; the telltale story of the *Ten Little Indians*.

"What else do you know about McGivney?"

"Simon was stationed in Iraq: 2005, I think. Nice fellow, quiet, very much antisocial. His dwelling is at the top of the cliffs overlooking the ocean. I did check Simon's place out, to see if I could find a clue to his whereabouts. Nothing seemed out of the ordinary, for the exception of one thing."

"What was that?" Steel asked.

"Simon's high-powered rifle up and vanished. I looked everywhere for it. I'm certain he kept his shooter in a trophy case next to the fireplace."

Ben responded, "Do you recall what type it might have been?"

"I believe it was an AWSM. Can't imagine how he smuggled one back from Iraq."

Ames said, "Sheriff, if you'll kindly point the way, Ben and I will take a ride to his residence and have a look around."

"You won't find anything."

"I don't expect we will, but it's just one of those things that go with the job. You know how it is with one's superiors; they'll have your ass in a sling, if you don't follow procedure."

"I hear you loud and clear. It'll only take me a minute to draw a sketch that will take you directly to his door. It was ajar when I checked out his place; didn't know what to make of it."

After he finished the scribbled drawing, Hayes said, "Keep me posted fellas. Right now Shire Latham wants me to display some welcome signs up and down Main Street. Have you bought your raffle tickets yet? They're going like hot cakes. Incidentally, watch your footing on the crag. It's a long drop down into the ravine, nothing but rocks."

McGivney's Place

It took about twenty minutes to drive up the zig-zag incline to Simon McGivney's lodge which stood relatively close to an elevated escarpment of terrain overlooking the mischievous sea. Longships lighthouse appeared much smaller when one observed it from a long distance. Matt had the sudden notion that the massive structure was daring the tempestuous waves to knock the eye-seeing bastion off its fortified pedestal. To think he and his partner had the nerve to climb that flashing monstrosity from within a few meters of the top. Fortunately, when they had, the sea was relatively in a tranquil mood.

As the Scotland Yard detectives approached McGivney's cabin, the opened door swayed monotonously in the swirling breeze. Matt wondered why Sheriff Hayes hadn't secured the entrance. Rupert had a number of idiosyncrasies, but so did everyone else Ames believed. Perhaps it was the many years he spent on the job that made Matt notice things as he did.

Steel pointed to Simon's trophy case and said, "That's where McGivney must have kept his AWSM."

"Ben, this facility hardly fits the description of our serial killer's base of operations. There's no evidence of writing materials, no computer, and no phone; where's the telly? From what I'm looking at- Simon's not our man. I'd bet my last shilling he's what everyone cracked him up to be, a simple recluse who happened to like fishing and reportedly owned an AWSM."

Matt moved closer to the window and said, "This is where the sniper must have taken a pop shot at us yesterday. You can see recently made scratches on the sill where he propped up his magnum."

Ben recorded everything Matt was saying.

While checking out the rifle's receptacle, Ames mused, "Sheriff Hayes must have flunked his 101 weapons exam."

"How so?"

"McGivney probably owned a Russian AK 46 or 47."

"What makes you think that?"

"The encasement is too small. No AWSM could have been housed in that contraption."

"Then maybe whoever shot at us used an AK instead."

"He couldn't have. Its effective range is only 400 meters. The AWSM Winchester Magnum has an effective range of over a thousand meters, and its kin, the AWSM Lapua Magnum, has an effective range of approximately 1500 meters."

"Should we confront Hayes about this?"

"No, we'll just ask Superintendent Carter to have Sheriff Rupert Hayes thoroughly checked out. In the mean time you and I will watch him like a hawk, as though our lives depended upon it."

While the two law officers proceeded in the direction of their vehicle, Matt noticed a low flying airplane heading straight toward them. It couldn't have been more than twenty meters above ground as it passed over their heads.

Ben ducked low and said, "If that's the serial killer, Matt, we're dead meat."

"Not to worry, this particular criminal mind is not ready to deal with us until it's absolutely time for the final curtain to come down. Hopefully we'll soon be in a better position to anticipate precisely when that will happen. Our present aerial visitors were sent by Superintendent Carter. Sorry, I did mean to tell you. So many things have been going on in my head at once. They're taking vertical photographs to capture images of the terrain."

"So why then is the aircraft returning in our direction?"

"I suppose they need to take some low angle shots. Ben, they're on *our* side. Wave to them."

As the single engine craft approached the two detectives, the pilot tipped its wings and flew off. Ben sounded pensive when he said, "Matt, do you think we're going to survive this case?"

"Perhaps yes, and then again, perhaps maybe not; in any event, this I know without a shadow of a doubt. If we don't have something to eat real soon, we're both likely to die from malnutrition."

CHAPTER 22

Sheriff Beware

After supper Ames encouraged his side-kick to get a good night's rest. In the meantime he would update Carter on all that transpired since they last spoke. When Marshall answered the phone, Matt thought to himself, *the man never sleeps!*

"Glad you called, Ames. I'm sensing the coroner's report will confirm that Parson Wingate and the headless corpsman are not one and the same."

"What makes you think so?"

"Thus far the serial killer has not produced a bona fide corpse. At the moment I believe he's having his 'kicks' on us. Once the bastard tires of his little game of charades, trust me, all hell will break loose- and in the process he'll skip town with us holding the bag. In the meantime try to get me a name that goes with that bloke who was fished out of the pond."

"Sounds logical, everything you said, Marshall; I need you to do a routine check on Sheriff Rupert Hayes. Try and find out if and when he left Heathrow Airport for the states, about three and a half weeks ago. I also need to know precisely when he returned. I suspect he knows much more than he's willing to say. He may even be somehow implicated in all this."

"A lawman, I can't believe it. These days you don't know *who* to trust."

"It's just that all the disappearances occurred during the time Hayes was supposedly out of town."

"I'll get right on it. Incidentally, Matt, a background check on all the missing persons, Wingate's profile sheet is still pending, came up clean for everyone, excepting for Simon McGivney's. While serving a stint in Iraq the bloke was dishonorably discharged for criminal negligence. Apparently he took it upon himself to pop off a few rounds of ammunition at the antagonists with his AWSM during a cease fire. Lucky for him he missed. At his Court Marshall hearing McGivney claimed he was on guard duty when he suspected the clowns were readying themselves to launch a bunch of rockets at the British command post to which he was assigned. That's about it. Draw your own conclusion."

Carter paused and then said, "One more thing, the aerial reconnaissance team found something. Check out a Mary Sweeny's place. She doesn't live too far from your hotel. Freshly cultivated soil has been detected on her property. You and Ben see to it, and let me know if the old biddy is collecting any three week old cadavers. Keep me posted. Don't have any more time for idle chatter." Click.

Steel was fast asleep when Ames entered their boarding house suite. Glancing at the dresser where Ben kept his note pad, Matt picked it up and thumbed through the pages. Of the numerous entries the constable made in the two days they arrived five notations caught the inspector's curios attention. They were very sketchy to say the least. *Toodle-oo, foul odor, Ten Little Indians, burns on hand* and *"some sheriff"* had been prominently circled.

Two last thoughts ran through Matt's mind before sleep overtook him. One was whether or not he'd make it to retirement, and the other pained him more deeply; namely, if anything happened to his youthful partner, he'd never forgive himself.

Coroner's Report

Mrs. Belldonger placed the morning newspaper on Matt and Ben's breakfast table. When Ames thanked her she said, "It's no bother, inspector, I know in your job one has to keep up with current events. I do hope the poor chap they fished from the pond wasn't Parson Wingate."

"Constable Steel and I will be getting an updated report from Coroner Quinton any moment now. We'll be sure to keep you posted."

"Thank you, inspector, I suppose there's nothing any of us can do but pray. Incidentally, gentlemen, the waitress serving the guest by the window, her name is Jessie, she'll be taking my place for a few days. My mum came down with a severe cold and I'm to look after the poor dear until she's feeling her old self again. Must get back to me job now, toodle-oo."

No sooner Mrs. Belldonger dashed off; the desk clerk delivered a verbal message to Matt. He informed Ames that Coroner Quinton would like to see him at his earliest convenience.

The Scotland Yard detectives received the lowdown from Larry Quinton. Carter called it right; the victim was not Parson Wingate. Whoever it was that got tossed out of the missing craft drowned before somehow being decapitated. The corpse apparently had an ICD, (Implanted Cardioverter Defibrillator). After the electronic code in the pacemaker was verified, Thomas Sims, a retired clergyman, was identified as the dead man found in the sea. When asked by Steel if the coroner noticed any sign of burns on either of the cadaver's hands, Quinton said he hadn't and that the evidence clearly indicated that the deceased had definitely been run over by a motor boat after he had already drowned.

As they left the morgue Ben said, "Matt, there's not a shred of tangible evidence anyone in this town was either murdered or ushered away against his or her free will."

"That's why the shire's decision to carry on business as usual suggests to me tourism outranks one unexplained drowning and six missing persons. Incidentally, Carter wants us to look up a Mary Sweeney."

"Who's Mary Sweeney?"

"According to Carter, I spoke to him after you retired last night; hers was the only recently disturbed property in the approximate area where a half dozen bodies could have possibly been buried. At least that's what aerial surveillance photos indicated."

"Matt," Ben asked, "Do you think this bloke, Sims, was murdered?"

"Suddenly, I don't know what to think. Who knows?"

In a melodramatic mimic, Ben responded, *"Only the shadow knows."*

Ames came back with, "Constable, you're beginning to sound more like a Yank every day. Let's go see Mary Sweeny, and before you get cute; I'll say it for you. Let's hope she'll not be *quite contrary.*"

At that Ben could not resist. Expecting a jab from his partner, he held this forearms before his chest and head as a protective shield as he hurriedly retorted, 'Or hope she doesn't possess a slew of sheep whose *fleeces are white as snow.*"

Spontaneously caught off guard they each gave one another a high five.

C H A P T E R   2 4

Mary Sweeney's Place

A beautiful array of flowers greeted the detectives. Mary Sweeney's front garden exuded a variety of odours that excelled whatever artificial perfumes were touted at Harrods, Harvey Nichols, or any of London's finer department stores. As the unexpected visitors approached the porch steps of her quaint stone cottage, the aging spinster greeted them while continuing to rock her rickety chair to and fro.

"Hello, gentlemen, is there anything I can do for you?"

"Mrs. Sweeney, my name is Inspector Matthew Ames from Scotland Yard, and this is my partner, Constable Benjamin Steel. We're here to ask you a few routine questions."

"What is it you would like to know? I haven't done anything wrong, have I; at least I don't think I have?"

"No Mary, that's not why we're here. Constable and I are presently engaged in assisting Sheriff Hayes in making inquiries pertaining to Parson Wingate's mysterious disappearance. Do you mind if we look around your premises? It'll only take a few minutes. Without having to say, you have a magnificent garden."

"Why thank you, inspector, I've just had Mr. Clyde Jamison, my neighbor, till my backyard. Next week he's going to plant a variety of perennials for me. I simply adore flowers, don't you?"

'I can't imagine what our fair country would be without them."
Ames couldn't think of anything else to say.

Captivated by Matt's obvious appreciation of horticulture, Mrs.
Sweeney said, "While you and your friend take care of whatever it is
you came here to do, I'll put the kettle on."

One quick glance at the freshly tilled earth assured Ames that
nothing more than a typical plowing of soil had been in progress. Steel
inquired, "Shouldn't we at least dig up a few patches here and there?"

"The earth has been evenly farmed. No, everything looks too
dignified. If anyone had recently been laid to rest here, there would be
evidence of scavenges having left their trademark. Ben, let's have a brief
chat with our hostess; besides, I'm quite in the mood for a soothing cup
of English tea."

Mary Sweeney spoke openly and was most cordial to the Scotland
Yard Detectives. During the course of conversation she discussed her
failing eyesight and that she lived all her life in Coventry Gardens. Mrs.
Sweeney also expressed her fondness and concern for Parson Wingate.
Finally, she mentioned that she didn't know what she'd do if it weren't
for Mrs. Melanie Belldonger, how her neighbor was always there for her.

Once Belldonger's name was brought up, it rang a bell. Waiting to get
first-hand information on the woman, Ames said, "Mary, I understand
Melanie's mum has contracted a severe cold. Mrs. Belldonger told Ben
and me she plans to spend quality time with her for at least a few days."

"That's strange; Melanie never mentioned anything to me about
leaving Coventry Gardens."

"Doesn't her mother live nearby, Ben asked?"

"Heaven's no, Mrs. Belldonger's mum used to live in a London
assisted living facility. I can't rightfully recall the name of the place.
You see my memory isn't as sharp as it used to be. However, there is one
thing that I haven't forgotten."

"What would that be, Mary?" Ames noted that Ben's voice was soft and endearing, as though a compassionate son had been speaking to his mother.

"Constable, Mrs. Evelyn Brister died three years ago."

The two detectives bade Mary Sweeney good-bye, and as they left the premises, Ben said to Matt, "I can't believe my ears. Melanie Belldonger flat out lied to us; she should be arrested."

"Maybe so, but not for telling us a falsehood about her mother; however, what Mary just said does give us sufficient reason to put our friendly maid-servant under a microscope. In any event, it's a loose end Carter will have to address."

CHAPTER 25

Searching for Clues

Shire Latham and the Scotland Yard detectives crossed paths at the entrance of Sheriff Hayes's front door. "Good day, gentlemen," Reed said, "have either of you seen the sheriff?"

"Why no," Matt answered, "but we can take a peep inside and see if he left a message for either of us."

After looking around and not finding any signs of Hayes, the shire said, "Rupert can be most anywhere. Kindly inform him that I need to speak to him at his earliest convenience." Half turning he paused and said, "I don't mean to sound insensitive, but until we have absolute evidence that any of our citizens have been forcibly detained or harmed, well, uh, the tourist season simply cannot be compromised. Inspector, you must understand, Larry Quinton did assure me that yesterday's unfortunate incident appeared to be quite accidental."

Matt spoke in a composed manner. "Mr. Latham, Scotland Yard does understand. I'll be sure to relay your message to Sheriff Hayes the moment he returns."

"Thank you, I'd hate to think what the consequences might be if Thomas Sim's death had been deemed a homicide. Good day, gentlemen." At that he left. Theoretically, much of what Reed said made sense, at least from a financial point of view.

Matt and Ben continued to take up where they left off in examining Jessica O'Brien's file. After several minutes of scanning the school teacher's personal effects, Ben said, "Matt, what do you think of this poem?

It's titled, *Before* and *After*.

> *God's gifts to mankind-*
> *Nature's wonders.*
> *Sweet dawn of light,*
> *Unruffled streams,*
> *Virgin wilderness,*
> *Fruit of the vine*
> *Paradise,*
> *Unending life.*

Then she goes on to say: *Adam's antiphon-*

> *Distrust,*
> *Moon-madness,*
> *Broken bridges,*
> *Mushroom clouds*
> *Smoldering torches,*
> *Aftermath,*
> *Undying death.*"

"It sounds like she's referring to God's creation and the consequences of sin, anything else?"

"Only that Jessica planned to visit Longships lighthouse at the time she was reportedly missing. According to what she says here, O'Brien needed inspiration to write a second stanza to a poem she had already started. It's titled Longships Lighthouse."

"I'd like to hear that first stanza," Matt retorted.

> *"Watchtower of might*
> *Sturdy, unshaken,*
> *Standing strong*
> *Amid ceaseless swells*
> *Of nature's persistent wrath.*
> *Unmoved, indomitable,*
> *Withstanding the irrevocable*
> *Onslaught of swirling sea.*
> *Majestic, towering, unrelenting*
> *All seeing eye,*
> *Hail to thee*
> *O British Isle's Beacon of Hope!"*

"Interesting, that's where McGivney supposedly bought it."

"Right on and where you and I almost bought it; don't forget."

"Ben, wasn't Peter Clayton a lighthouse keeper?"

"I've got it right here, yep, Pendeen Lighthouse. Let's see, it's just north of us. I believe it's visible from Doc Hardy's place. Why do you ask?"

"It appears another common factor is beginning to emerge."

Ben said, "Thomas Sims was found in close proximity to Longships lighthouse, but how does Peter Clayton fit into the scheme of things?"

"Longships lighthouse is unmanned. I'd imagine it would only require occasional maintenance. Someone has to do it; why not Peter Clayton?"

"Matt, what's your point?"

"My point is that there appears to be a correlation between Longships lighthouse and several of our missing subjects."

The ring of the telephone interrupted the two detectives. Picking up the receiver, Matt said, "Inspector Ames, here."

"Matt, it's Carter. What do you have for me?"

"The coroner's report just came in; you were right, Marshall, the corpse wasn't Winsgate's. Apparently, a local retired clergyman, Thomas Sims, accidentally drowned. His decapitation was caused by the propeller of someone else's boat. Marshall, see if you can find out anything on a Lawrence Quinton, a Melanie Belldonger and (whether her mum, Evelyn Brister) is still kicking, and a Reed Latham; also, any news on Hayes?"

"We should be receiving a report on him very shortly. Right now, however, due to a power outage, the communications system is caput."

"Just to let you know, Ben and I didn't find anything suspicious at Mary Sweeney's place. He and I are going to finish up here, have something to eat, and then do some reconnoitering. Be sure your team puts a rush on those names I just gave you. And, Marshall, find out what you can about Thomas Sims, the bloke who lost his head the other night. I'm curious to know why he was wearing his rabat."

From the other end Ames heard Carter bark, "Yes, *sir*. At your service *sir*. Is there anything else, *sir?* You're getting to be one big pain in my ass, *sir*. And another thing, what the hell is a rabat?"

"It's a black cloth a parson wears on his shirt front to signify he's a clergyman."

"Is that so? For a minute I thought you were talking about a bunny. You know, a bunny, as in bunny rabbit." Click.

CHAPTER 26

Melanie Reflects

The Penzance train terminal reminded Mrs. Belldonger of a swarm of ants coming and going every which way. *Tourists,* she thought to herself. Before climbing aboard the London Cross Country Express, Melanie said to the porter. "Be careful with my trunk; won't you?"

"Yes, madam, would you like me to tag and check that other piece of luggage? It looks like it may be a little too cumbersome for you to carry on the train."

Removing a quid from her purse, she said, "That won't be necessary. It contains delicacies, and I'd have much more peace of mind if it remained with me. Here, this is for you."

With a gratuitous smile the redcap nodded his head, ticketed the robust woman's luggage, and proceeded to take it to the baggage car. Soon the express left the station and proceeded to speed its way to London. Comfortably settled in her berth, Melanie casually looked out the window and stared into oblivion. She focused her attention on the missing Coventry Gardens citizens she knew so well.

Simon McGivney pervaded her thoughts. It's true; he was sort of strange, living by himself and all, but whenever he stopped at the boarding house for an occasional breakfast, he always portrayed friendliness in his demeanor. Whatever became of him, she wondered? It didn't seem quite right. Though he was deemed a recluse by some of the villagers, surely Simon would have told *her* if he intended to take a holiday.

Peter Clayton and Melanie were closest of friends. Whatever secrets the co-workers shared remained confidential. There could only be one reason why he didn't speak to her before he went off without saying good-bye. Mrs. Belldonger removed a tissue from her purse and patted her teary eyes. She couldn't bring herself to dwell upon what she suspected.

Jessica O'Brien, you couldn't meet a sweeter person. She loved children and wrote the most beautiful pastoral poems. The paraplegic school teacher lived close by and had been a consolation to Melanie, especially at the time Mrs. Belldonger's mother fell victim to Alzheimer's disease before she had to be institutionalized. Melanie contemplated she had made the right decision in not telling anyone of Evelyn's passing a few years back.

Edgar Stevenson had no relatives. He was such a kindly gentleman. Though she and Edgar were never more than fair-weather friends, someone would most certainly have shared with her whatever it was that made him suddenly disappear. There could be only one explanation for what had happened to him. Right now she didn't want to think about it. Once again Melanie suppressed her worst suspicions.

Dr. David Hardy came to mind. What a marvelous human being! It wasn't like him to leave town without informing her of his taking leave. Poor Doc, whatever became of him? More tears.

And then there was Parson Wingate. Melanie knew him only too well. Unmistakably, Nathaniel was very much alive and up to his old tricks. Oh, how she wished their paths never crossed. Another sudden burst of tears returned, and Melanie briskly wiped them away.

Finally, sitting upright, she confronted her next wave of thoughts with a verbal self admonishment, "Why didn't I share my worst fears with those nice detectives? I'm sure they would have understood and not held me accountable. Melanie Belldonger, shame on you."

And with that she reached into her carry-on bag, pulled out some unfinished embroidery and began to crochet. There was absolutely no sense for her to continue crying over spilt milk.

CHAPTER 27

Dishonor among Thieves

As he and Steel were heading out to lunch, Ames heard a noise emanating from Sheriff Hayes's office. Entering the partially opened door, Matt noticed Rupert sifting through a pile of papers strewn upon his desk. The Scotland Yard inspector said, "Shire Reed's been asking for you. He appeared to be bent out of shape about something."

Before he could acknowledge Ames, the phone rang. Hayes picked up the receiver. Recognizing the sheriff's voice the caller whispered, "Rupert, we've been had. After you check the contents of your safe, come straight over. Melanie Belldonger played us for a couple of saps. The bitch high-tailed it to London, and she has with her our share of the money to boot."

Attempting to remain unnerved, the sheriff retorted into the phone, "Inspector Ames just now said you wanted to see me. Yes, I'll be there right away," and he hung up.

"Ben and I wanted you to join us for lunch at Terry's, but I see you're up to your eyeballs with Latham."

"You got that right. Thanks, inspector, but I'll have to take a rain check. I better see what Reed wants before he has a canary."

"Duty before pleasure; we'll catch each other up to speed later."

As Matt and Steel was about to leave, the telephone rang in Ames's office. "I'll get it," Ben said. "Why don't you go ahead and I'll join you after I'm done with Cater? Perhaps the network is back on line, and he's calling to let us know."

No sooner had the Scotland Yard officers disappeared from view; Rupert locked his office door and removed a quaint, pastoral picture from the wall. Upon opening the exposed cylindrical safe, his complexion reddened. It was empty. Whatever his share of the gross receipts he and the others extorted from the hamlet's tourist industry for the past three years had up and vanished. At least the sheriff knew who took it and in which direction she was headed.

Fearing the Scotland Yard detectives may still be on the premises; Hayes bolted out the back door and sprinted to Shire Latham's office. The irate sham of a lawman had sensed from the very beginning Melanie Belldonger could not be trusted. As was in his heart to do he'd get even with the two-timer, and her punishment would be much more than a slap on the wrist.

Reed was speaking on the intercom when Hayes slipped into the side entrance. "Gwen, call helipad center and inform Forester to have the eggbeater fully fueled and ready for immediate take off." Reed then clicked off and said to Rupert, "I've been trying to get in touch with you all morning. From the look on your face Melanie swindled you too."

"How'd she do it?" Sheriff Hayes was visibly upset.

"I've been thinking about it. In a way it makes sense. From the very beginning she must have planned on double-crossing us. Why else would she cajole us into believing that all the free breakfasts she's been shuffling back and forth stemmed from the goodness of her heart? Her shrewd trickery enabled Melanie to have access in locating our vault codes. She had to have made impressions of our latchkeys to craft duplicates by using the boarding house locksmith cutting machine. Belldonger then carefully chose an opportune time to rip us off before she split. I'd say those Scotland Yard detectives spooked her. Instead of risking the chance of seeing everything go down hill, she must have panicked and decided to bolt."

In somewhat of a quandary Hayes said, "So what'll we do now?"

"Rupert, you and I can still intercept Melanie before she reaches her destination. As luck would have it, I ascertained from Wade Timmons, who works at the Penzance train depot, that our nemesis purchased a ticket to Victoria Station and boarded the London Express. That's when I got a little suspicious and started checking into things." Reed paused to look at his watch and said, "Belldonger's train left a little over an hour ago."

"Latham, how do you suppose Melanie will leave the country? She'd be a fool not to fly the coup in a hurry."

"I suspect she'll take the earliest cruise ship leaving London Harbor. She hates to fly."

"Reed, any scrutiny into either of our lives will spell doomsville."

"This is why we're through talking here. Melanie Belldonger has our money and there's barely enough time to head her off. Is Ames and that constable of his still in the office?"

"I believe they were heading out to lunch."

"Good, we haven't a minute to lose. After we've taken care of business with Melanie at Victoria Station, I know someone who will give us safe passage to Brussels. We can either hang together or split, whichever you prefer. The copter should be refueled by now, so let's get cracking. Rupert, it's needless to say what else has to be done."

"You don't have to concern yourself with Belldonger. After we retrieve the money she stole from us, well, she'll just have to get used to pushing up daisies."

"You've got the spare keys to the chopper?"

"I always carry them with me."

Rather than reflecting upon their immediate predicament with careful deliberation, the two Coventry Gardens highly esteemed officials commenced a spontaneous journey that, instead of hopefully ending up on Easy Street, would take a turn in an unforeseen, bizarre direction.

CHAPTER 28

Third Time's a Charm

While Ames waited for Steel to show up for lunch, he procured a table and ordered an iced tea. It was then he noticed a handsome looking woman eyeing him. The inspector's heart skipped a beat when the patron exposed her slender legs in the process of standing up to leave. Surprisingly, the fair haired lady turned, looked at Matt, and smiled. Walking over to him she said, "I don't mean to be intrusive, but I wondered if I might have a word with you."

"Be my guest." Ames said, "Won't you sit down, Ms…"

"Hamilton, Ms. Tracey Hamilton. My waiter pointed you out to me when I asked him if he knew someone who would be able to help me find a missing person. From what he said, Sheriff Hayes never seems to be around when you need him. Lucky for me you just walked in."

Matt stood up, took her extended hand, and said, "I'm Scotland Yard Inspector Matthew Ames. Won't you sit down? May I order you a drink?"

"No thank you, inspector; I've just eaten."

Ames noticed Tracy placing a paperback edition of Robert Frost's poems on the table. He said, "Frost, he's my favorite American poet."

"He's my grandmother's favorite as well. When I was a little girl she used to recite to me *Stopping by Woods on a Snowy Evening,* especially at bedtime. The words have a soothing cadence, like a lullaby."

Matt curiously asked, "Your grandmother, who might she be?"

"Jessica O'Brien. You see, inspector. . ."

"Call me Matt," Ames insisted.

"You see, Matt, I just arrived yesterday, and not finding Sheriff Hayes to inquire about Jessica's absence, someone at the tourist bureau told me that she apparently left town without telling anyone where she was going. I'm extremely worried. Mrs. O'Brien did expect me yesterday. Surely my grandmother would have informed me, if she had intentions of leaving town."

"Where, might I ask, are you staying right now?"

"At Nana's house, where I always do when I come to visit her; why do you ask?"

"May I suggest you relocate your present residence to the Pendleton Hotel; that is, until we locate Mrs. O'Brien? I don't mean to alarm you, but unofficially your grandmother's house is currently being treated as a crime scene."

"Is my grandmother in any sort of danger? What's happened to her? Where is she? Matt, please tell me, if something's terribly wrong, I need to know."

"To be straightforward Mrs. O'Brien is among a few Coventry Gardens townsfolk who are reportedly unaccounted for. This is why Scotland Yard deemed it necessary for my partner, Constable Benjamin Steel, and me to look into things. We're doing everything possible to find out what's become of them."

"I'll do as you ask, Matt, but I assure you, I'm not faint of heart. I won't leave Coventry Gardens until I learn the truth of Nana's whereabouts."

"Tracey, Ben and I have our temporary headquarters set up in one of Sheriff Hayes's spare rooms. After you've settled in at the hotel, feel free to stop by, won't you? Incidentally, we've just finished examining Jessica's personal effects. We thought they may perhaps assist us in our investigation."

"And have they helped you?"

"Actually, it's difficult to say. Later, come by the office. Maybe after perusing some of Mrs. O'Brien's recent poems you'll feel less apprehensive. She's truly a passionate writer."

"Thank you, it won't take me very long to procure a room at the hotel. I truly appreciate all you're doing to locate my grandmother." Grasping Ames by the forearm she exclaimed, "Matt, please find her." Tracey then abruptly left the table, paid her bill, and hurried out the door.

Steel, who had entered the restaurant moments before, sat down across from Matt. He spoke in a gentle voice, "Nice dish, who is she?"

Omitting to address the question, Matt answered, "I wouldn't mind being her best friend."

"You know what they say, partner," remembering what Ames had told him on the train, that he had been twice divorced, "third time's a charm."

Enthralled by her natural appeal, Matt replied, "The lady's name is Tracey Hamilton, Ms. Tracey Hamilton. She's Jessica O'Brien's granddaughter. So tell me what has Marshall have to say?"

Disregarding his partner's lingering preoccupation with the standout woman's physical attributes, Ben said, "The big news is- Sheriff Hayes or someone using his credentials deplaned before the aircraft departed Heathrow for the U.S. of A. nearly four weeks ago. Apparently the bloke had some sort of seizure just as the plane approached the runway for take off."

Ignoring routine procedure, Sheriff Hayes and Shire Latham boarded the Lands End utility helicopter. Before anyone could prevent the machine from lifting off, Rupert propelled it into the sky.

Upon its ascent, an on duty service operator quickly set his lunch aside and yelled over to someone entering the communications center. "Have dispatch contact that bozo in the whirlybird. He needs to get his ass back down here, pronto. It's just been reported the chopper has a faulty rotor system. The blades are apt to seize up. I haven't had a chance to refuel it yet!"

CHAPTER 29

Death in Disguise

Gazing out the window of his tour bus the Coventry Gardens serial killer smiled curiously. If everything went according to plan, this would be Superintendent Marshall Carter's last day of existence. The psychopath appeared to be dressed like an ordinary constable, however he did mask himself with a thick moustache, lengthy sideburns and a distinguished looking goatee. Dark glasses tended to screen the maverick's eyes.

As commuter vehicles intermingled with streams of heavy traffic, hoards of pedestrians hustled past the majestic New Scotland Yard metropolis in Victoria. At the stroke of noon the red double-decker charter bus slowly pulled up to a reserved parking area. While sightseeing passengers disembarked amid their gaiety, the disguised police officer discreetly blended among the crowd. A badge issued by Vintage Tour Lines conspicuously clung to everyone's outerwear. The pseudonym on the imposter's jacket read: *Brandt Moore*, a random name he retrieved from a local telephone directory. Within minutes the eager visitors entered the renowned law enforcement complex.

As usual a routine metal detector security scan was enforced. Anyone wearing the tour line identification logo was ushered through a second set of iron gates without additional delay. A woman's voice then echoed from a mini microphone attached to her navy blue tailored suit.

"Ladies and gentlemen, welcome to New Scotland Yard headquarters. My name is detective Cindy Mason, and I will be your tour guide for the next hour. Sorry to say, due to an extraordinary high volume of events, today's tour will consist of two brief infomercial productions, rather than the normally scheduled walk through procedure. However, I promise you will not be disappointed. So let's get started. This way please."

The group was then escorted to a small amphitheater on the third floor where it was seated before a semi-circular stage that exhibited a concave screen. First, an interesting thirty minute video, depicting how Scotland Yard changed its image through the years, captivated the audience. Then a gruesome slide show followed. It brought gasps of horror to the viewers when surreal pictures of Jack the Ripper's victims flashed upon the screen. The audio that accompanied the exhibition had been similarly shocking and successfully managed to give Moore his money's worth of excitement.

In winding things up Cindy Mason said, "As previously mentioned, due to an unpredictable high volume of activity, our forensic department has been deemed a restricted area and, unfortunately, the same holds true for our scheduled visit to Superintendent Marshall Carter's headquarters which happens to be located just above my head. I deeply do apologize for any inconvenience our abbreviated tour caused any of you. We'll now move to the elevators to our right which will take us to ground level where light refreshments will be served. Before returning to the bus each of you will receive a packet of literature which I believe will answer whatever general questions you may still have. Thank you, everyone, for sharing part of your day with New Scotland Yard. We've enjoyed having you with us."

Brandt Moore noticed a sign that gave him a sigh of relief. It read: THESE STAIRS ARE FOR PERSONNEL USE ONLY. He moved closer to it, paused, and patiently waited.

CHAPTER 30

May Day

Having downed a quick lunch, the two lawman thought it best to see if Carter had any updated news to analyze. Prior to reaching the office, they heard a distinct sputtering sound emanating from almost directly above. The whirlybird's chaotic swirling motion immediately confirmed it was in dire distress. Shielding their eyes from the midday sun, several pedestrians paused to look up.

"Look! Over there," someone pointed. Be as it may, the utility helicopter with Sheriff Hayes and Shire Latham aboard suddenly appeared high above the launch pad from which it had taken off only a short while ago.

"It's out of control!" another shouted.

Screams of disbelief were coming from every direction. "My God, it's going to crash!"

"Someone, call an ambulance."

"This can't be happening."

"God, help us. Somebody, do something!"

"Have mercy, oh Lord."

The copter twisted and wavered a few more times before it nose-dived sharply to the ground. Sparse clouds of smoke spewed into the air. In an instant it was over, excepting for the lamentations and bewildering cries that lingered among those who witnessed, first hand, a most horrifying event they'd much sooner forget.

Ben looked at Matt and said in a subdued voice, "If it's who I think it might be in that whirlybird, it could very well be that our phantom search, for you know who, has come to a screeching halt."

"Hayes? Maybe so, partner, but we can never assume anything. Call Carter and tell him what happened. I'll see what I can find out."

"Partner, I can't believe it, but right now I think I'm going to be sick."

"Before you do, constable, I strongly suggest you call Carter first."

CHAPTER 31

Suspicions Confirmed

It didn't take very long for Matt Ames to be briefed on what precipitated the bizarre accident that occurred at the heliport. On the scene witnesses observed Sheriff Hayes and Shire Latham climb aboard the copter before anyone could stop them. The craft had just returned from West Cornwall Hospital in Penzance and, aside from being extremely low on fuel, it needed to be serviced for rotor system repairs. Both occupants were killed minutes after take-off. No one could account as to why two seasoned pilots did not adhere to proper aeronautic procedures.

Melanie Belldonger looked at her watch. Just as she did, the conductor's guttural voice resounded outside her door. "We'll be pulling into Victoria Station in twenty minutes, folks, please have your luggage tickets in hand when you disembark."

"Here already?" The heavy-set passenger from Coventry Gardens was again talking softly to herself. "Such a pity Mum passed away when she did. If she were alive today, we'd be packing off to California together. Brochures don't lie. It's such a lovely place in which to lose oneself among the upper crust. I must remember to write a postcard to my former partners. Oh there I go again, getting ahead of myself."

CHAPTER 32

Intruder Within

Brandt Moore stood by the stairway that led directly to Superintendent Carter's office. When the two service elevators stopped to take the tour group down to the lobby, it was then the deceitful intruder disappeared from the others without being noticed. He paused at the next landing and composed himself. Extricating a shoulder pouch from within his jacket, he slung it around his head and arm. Brandt then removed a few phony dispatches from the tan leather bag.

Taking a deep breath, Moore opened the door and casually turned to his right. Luck was with him. The large print on the door to his left read:

EXECUTIVE DIRECTOR

SUPERINTENDENT MARSHALL CARTER

Placing his hand into a pouch, the serial killer felt for the sharply carved ivory dagger. Shielding it from view, he would then enter the room, approach his target with a handful of bogus dispatches; and at the precise moment Carter reached for them, Moore would plunge the lethal weapon into the police chief's carotid artery.

To Ames's surprise Tracey Hamilton was sitting across from his desk when he returned from the heliport. She immediately jumped up and said, "Ben told me what happened. Matt, is it true? Was Sheriff Hayes in that awful accident?"

"Tracey, where's Constable Steel?"

Not answering him the distraught woman hurried over to Matt, fell into His opened arms, and wept. Removing a handkerchief from his pocket, Ames delicately blotted the moisture from her eyes. It was then Ben entered the room.

"Ben, I need to speak to Carter."

Steel shook his head before saying, "I'm afraid that won't be possible, partner, his phone just keeps ringing." Sensing he had interrupted a tender moment, Ben turned away to leave Matt and Tracey to themselves.

Ames didn't really wan't to talk to Carter. He was at the threshold of his retirement and fed up playing cat-and-mouse with a sadistic killer he'd much rather see dead than alive. The assignment was tedious, incomprehensible, and overwhelmingly frustrating. Two more people who may have been tied to the case had bitten the dust. For all that transpired, since he and Steel were assigned to the case, they were back to square one.

Right now the distraught detective wanted nothing more than to squeeze Tracey Hamilton in his arms and caress her with an embrace that would last forever. It happened to be the unmistakable truth. They bonded the very first moment their eyes met in Terrys. Matt knew it and strongly suspected Tracey felt the same way. His impeccable intuitive spirit confirmed it. Imagine that. Ben was right. Third time around *is* a charm. How wonderful! How charmingly beautiful!

Hamilton looked up at Ames. She could feel her heart throb faster. Words could not express her emotions. Drawing Matt closer, their lips touched ever so tenderly. They kissed again, and then again. Amazingly, after having just met and hardly knowing anything about the other, Tracey and Matt, without having to say, were deeply lost in the sea of love.

CHAPTER 33

Narrow Escape

Brandt Moore found himself in a precarious position. Not finding Carter there he needed to get out of the office fast. However, the would–be killer noticed a memo on Marshall's desk and quickly perused the message. Its contents immediately quelled his fears. Turning the knob he slowly opened the door and stepped into the corridor. Just as he was leaving by the stairwell Brandt had used before, a voice stopped him in his tracks. "We're not supposed to use the stairs unless it's an emergency."

"Oh, I didn't know," Moore spoke in a composed voice. "I somehow got separated from Detective Cindy Mason's tour group."

"This is a restricted area. What's your name? No one without clearance should be on this floor. How'd you get up here?"

"I'm with Vintage Tour Lines. As you can see, I'm dressed for the occasion. I needed to use the men's room. The tour was scheduled to see Superintendent Carter. Where did everyone go?"

"You're too late. Superintendent Carter has left for the day."

"Do you know when he'll be back? The tourists were so much looking forward to meeting him."

"Sorry, that's classified information."

It was then the elevator paused at the fourth floor. Brandt's cleverly worded schmooze convinced the detective that Moore had been obviously separated from his tour group; so he casually escorted him to the main foyer. When the elevator reached its destination, a familiar voice hollered, "Hurry up, Mr. Moore, our bus is about to leave. We're holding up traffic."

Brandt Moore's short-circuited imagination had him boiling over with glee. Recalling the note on Carter's desk, it read: *"In the event anyone wants to know, I can be reached at Coventry Gardens, wherever the hell that is."*

Well now, Moore mused, *I'll just have to dispose of the three of them all at once.*

CHAPTER 34

Admission of Love

At Matt's suggestion Tracey accepted his advice to procure lodging at the Pendlenton Hotel. He'd feel less apprehensive in knowing that, the woman whose mere acquaintance jolted him into believing there was more to life than merely living by oneself after retirement, she'd be at arm's distance of his protection. The serial killer's pattern of behavior did not fit any other criminal's description he'd ever witnessed. If someone else were to suddenly disappear, Ames would do everything in his power to not let it be Tracey Hamilton's name that next highlighted the missing persons list.

After she had departed, Ames went into the adjoining office and noticed Steel at the computer. He said, "Since when is it impossible for anyone to speak to Superintendent Carter; the man never sleeps?"

"According to his last email," Ben answered, "the boss is having someone fly the company monoplane down here, with him on it."

Flippantly, Ames blurted out, "That's all we need right now is another…" He paused and then added, "Sorry, partner, I don't even want to go there."

"Matt, do you think Carter knows about Hayes and Latham?"

"It's probably the reason he's flying out. Lands End heliport center advised me they sent a communiqué to Scotland Yard minutes after the copter hit the ground."

"Why should that light a fire under Carter?"

"Because he may have reason to believe we're next."

In an attempt not to focus on his partner's train of thought, Ben said, "I was just about to have a cup of tea, Matt. Would you like some? I'm kind of anxious to know a little more about Tracey Hamilton, Ms. Tracey Hamilton."

"You mean Tracey Hamilton and me."

"Of course, what else did you think I meant?"

"Really, Ben, there's not much to say about Tracey, excepting that I've completely fallen head over heels for her."

"That's cool. What do you say we have a real drink to that?"

"Hell no, and lose my pension? You know Carter; he's got a nose like a beagle. Constable Steel, when this case is over you and I…"

"And Tracey," Ben quickly injected.

"And Tracey, the three of us will drink Patty O'Doul's dry. In the mean time let's straighten up this office. You know how meticulous the boss is."

"Yeah, I know, I's dotted and T's crossed. A whole lot of bull shit. Don't tell him I said that."

Melanie Belldonger's train pulled up to Victoria Station. Moore, still in his police outfit, approached the opposite platform where the next scheduled Express to Penzance was idling until its engineer received a signal from his conductor to depart. Brandt would then set off the time bomb he intended to use when all three Scotland Yard detectives were together, at a time they least expected their woeful surprise. Afterward, the psychopath anticipated he'd resume his lethal mission elsewhere, the United States perhaps, where lawlessness and disregard for human life was becoming a distinct pattern of behavior.

CHAPTER 35

Carter Surprises

After the office seemed tidy enough, and everything looked as it should, Inspector Ames and Constable Steel greeted their superintendent at Lands End's amphibious landing site. En route to Coventry Gardens Marshall Carter told his deputies that Scotland Yard uncovered dirty linen on Hayes and Latham; that if their past misdeeds were to ever have become public knowledge, they both would have been dismissed for lying under oath. More importantly, it was vital to find out what Rupert and Reed were up to before they died in the helicopter tragedy.

Furthermore, it had not been Rupert Hayes who disembarked from flight 117 at Heathrow Airport as previously reported. Forensic evidence confirmed that an alias, Osgood Townsend, had faked en epileptic fit and was taken to an emergency facility. He had evidently substituted his credentials with a phony set of documents bearing Hayes's name. It was Townsend who had arranged to make it appear that Rupert endeavored to cover up his tracks at the time Scotland Yard began receiving eerie letters of bizarre deaths taking place at Coventry Gardens. As it were, Osgood bolted from the care center where he'd been taken before any revelation of his true identity had been documented.

"However, we did catch a break," Carter was saying. "Forensics linked a latent fingerprint found on Townsend's gurney to an individual's by the name of Cameron Vogel. He'd been a patient in London's Monroe

Sanatorium at the time he escaped from the institution with the help of his nurse. Hold on to your hats, gentlemen. His accomplice was none other than Melanie Belldonger. Whatever other aliases he may have used to commit a crime in the past, if the fingerprints match Vogel's, we'll know they're connected to an escapee with a severe mental condition."

Steel injected. "Who would have ever believed? Then Sheriff Hayes was not responsible for any of the missing persons."

"Yes, constable, that is affirmative. Our agents in the U.S. have verified he'd been on flight 117 when it landed at Kennedy and that he returned to London three weeks later. Gentlemen, I believe the revelation of our phantom suspect is imminent. Scotland Yard has Vogel's prints on global alert. They're bound to coincide with someone who's been recently residing in this very township and quite familiar with Melanie Belldonger."

It was then Tracey Hamilton entered the office. Ames jumped up and said, "Superintendent Carter, this is Ms. Tracey Hamilton; she's in the process of finding out what became of her grandmother, Mrs. Jessica O'Brien- one of our missing persons."

The Chief of Police said, "Ms. Hamilton, I'm sorry the circumstances couldn't be more pleasanter. I give you my word; everything under the sun is being done to locate your grandmother and everyone else who has mysteriously disappeared from our midst."

"You're very kind, superintendent. Thank you." Tracey then turned to Ames and asked if she could peruse some of Jessica's recent poems.

Since the documents had already been scrutinized, Matt gathered the material Tracey requested and, handing the packet over to her, he said, "We may have further need of these."

"Thanks, Matt, it won't take me very long to get this back to you. Will I be seeing you later this evening?"

"Tomorrow will be better. I'm afraid recent developments will be keeping the three of us busy for a while."

"I understand." Pausing she added, "Gentlemen, I know you must have your plates full. Please know I'm extremely grateful for all that you are doing. Good luck in your mission. It was a terrible thing that happened earlier. I'll be sure to keep you all in my prayers." Turning to Ames, she softly uttered, "Be careful, Matt."

No sooner Tracey Hamilton departed; Carter said to Ames, "Nice woman, I like her. From the way you two looked at each other, I just might have my hands full here. Whatever, back to business; Constable Steel, kindly order some sandwiches from next door. I'll have ham and cheese on rye. I'm afraid we're going to be here until we're finished."

Matt quizzically looked at Ben and said, "I'll have the same."

"Well, what do you know?" Steel's voice bore a tinge of humor. "We three can agree on at least *one* thing."

"What's that?" Carter and Ames spoke in unison.

"Ham and cheese on rye," and with that, he shrugged his shoulders and left.

CHAPTER 36

Killer's Instinct

Before alighting from her train Melanie Belldonger waited for the traffic on the platform to dissipate. No sooner had she awkwardly stepped down with her cumbersome hand luggage a familiar personality caught sight of her. The woman instinctively looked up and their eyes interlocked. Despite his disguise, Brandt Moore knew in an instant that he had been recognized.

Melanie hurried along the side of the coach from which she had just disembarked. In a matter of seconds Moore gingerly hopped over the set of tracks separating the two trains and caught up to the fast moving matron. He then gently cradled the heavy-set woman around the waist. His voice was soothing, "Why are you in such a hurry, luv? You should know it isn't very sporting to ignore an old friend. What brings you to London, my sweet? We both know your mum passed away three years ago."

"Please do me no harm. After all we've been through, I could never betray you." Noticing her confronter's name tag, Mrs. Belldonger thought it best to address her former patient by his latest alias.

"Please, Mr. Moore," she again pleaded, "I've always stood by you, protected you. Surely you must know that. Of course, you do, luv. What do you say we have a cuppa, like we always used to? Come now; tell me how I can be of help."

Reaching for his sharp instrument, the one he intended to use on Superintendent Carter, Moore flashed the letter opener and said, "Melanie, it must be this way. Try to understand. The voices, they've returned."

Too frightened to scream the former nurse's notion that the malevolence hovering over her could truly be rehabilitated faded into oblivion. In shear desperation she implored, "I've got money, more money than you could ever dream of having. Please, it's the truth. I've never lied to you. You don't have to worry about a thing, luv. I have it right here, enough to last a lifetime. Take it. I swear, I won't say anything about having seen you."

Attempting to assert herself Mrs. Belldonger ranted on. "Mr. Moore, as I've told you repeatedly, don't pay any heed to those nasty voices. If you wish, I'll continue to take good care of you, like I always have."

Melanie then noticed the queer look in his eyes. She frantically searched for additional convincing words that would put Moore at ease, having done so many times in the past, ever since she'd been assigned to him. He had trusted her. He'll trust her again. Why hadn't the asylum been more sensitive, exhibited human compassion to its inmates, she often wondered?

In a flash, as though blindfolds had been suddenly ripped away from that part of her she fought so hard to suppress, Belldonger fully came to grips with the grave mistake she chose to deny all these years. Melanie abruptly hesitated, as though she were transporting her thoughts to the precise point in time she fell in love with a criminally insane patient by the name of Cameron Vogel.

It was after the veteran lass served a four year stint in the Middle East as a British Marine Corps sister that she had been appointed assistant head nurse of the psychiatric ward at London's Monroe Hospital. Cameron very much appeared to respond to Nurse Belldonger's amazing innovative mental retardation treatments.

Infatuation superceded common sense when Melanie, enraptured in her new found beau, assisted Vogel to escape from the sanatorium. The clever Florence Nightingale had done her homework. Before leaving

England she contacted a friend she met in the service and procured a job on the Isle of Sri Lanka where she spent the greater part of twelve years doing everything conceivably possible to quell the raging demons that incited Cameron to exhibit violent tendencies.

During this time, Vogel's abhorrent mental seizures subsided. Although he displayed continuous signs of normal behavior, he and Melanie pined for England. According to a British internet blog, an absentee landlord of the Pendleton Hotel in Coventry Gardens, a small tourist municipality near the coast of Lands End, was in dire need of a housekeeper. The shire of the same town was also looking for someone to fill a recent vacancy, one that Vogel believed he would be the perfect man for the job. Belldonger was ecstatic. She could not have asked for a safer haven for either of them, especially Cameron.

Before she left her nursing position at the sanatorium, days after Cameron Vogel escaped from the institution; Melanie regrettably resigned to take care of her invalid mother, so she said. The investigative report concluded that the patient in question apparently took advantage of a breach in the institution's security system. Neither nurse Belldonger nor anyone else was ever implicated in being a party to the incident.

During their return trip to England, on the final evening of their cruise, Melanie vividly relived the occasion- as though it occurred yesterday. Upon seeing Cameron dressed in his Masquerade Ball costume, she remembered saying, *"Why, you look like a thousands bucks, luv, where'd you get that neat outfit? It's absolutely you."*

"I kind of borrowed it from a bloke I met in the cocktail lounge. He said he wouldn't be needing it any more. Like you say, this outfit becomes me."

It wasn't until the cruise ship docked at Bristol that Melanie learned that a single male passenger had been unaccounted for. Though her sixth sense raised a red flag, she chose to dismiss the matter from her mind completely, until a number of her Coventry Gardens associates began to disappear.

She could see it in his eyes, those fiendish eyes. The man who now called himself Moore was beyond hope. Of course, he was incapable of perceiving things rationally. Yes, he'd been lucid for years, but Cameron

Vogel was nothing more or less than what his admittance papers declared him to be, an incurable psychopath.

If anyone lingering on the platform had taken notice of the couple, they'd have thought a police officer was caressing his wife after she'd returned from her journey. Unable to control his pent up anxieties Brandt Moore cupped one hand over the fearful woman's mouth and without hesitation plunged the ivory dagger into Melanie Belldonger's jugular vein. Shoving her stout body into the framework on the train's portal, the killer grabbed his victim's carry-on, made an about face, and zigzagged his way to the country express scheduled to depart for Penzance. It seemed as though the assailant's former lover and caretaker, who rescued him from the insane asylum, never meant a thing to him at all.

"All aboard!"

Having left his slain victim's personal diary in her waist pocket where she always kept it, Brandt Moore climbed onto the London Express moments before it exited the station. A serial killer unbeknown to all England, for the exception of a few individuals working for an impeccable law enforcement agency, was determined to finish what the demons in his head had ordained him to do.

/

CHAPTER 37

Steel's Conundrum

While Ben was ordering out and Matt was preoccupied on the phone, a local councilman stopped by the police station and asked Superintendent Carter if he would be gracious enough to say a few dignified words on behalf of the township at tomorrow afternoon's memorial service to honor Sheriff Hayes and Shire Latham. Although Marshall preferred not to oblige, should he have declined, it would be viewed as a mark of disrespect to everyone in the community. Carter, condescending to the request, sent the gentleman away with what appeared to be a look of satisfaction on his face.

After the detectives had eaten, the three concurred that the phantom serial killer, Cameron Vogel (alias Osgood Townsend) because of his close relationship with Melanie Belldonger, had been living among the missing persons all this time. The question remained, who in Coventry Gardens had once been admitted to the Monroe Sanatorium where Melanie once worked?

Carter was saying, "Forensics was able to eliminate everyone on the missing persons list as being a possible serial killer suspect, for the exception of one individual. The rascal must have stolen the identity of someone he first killed and then impersonated him with an alias."

After listening to Marshall's spiel, Matt injected, "Blimey, Chief, what you just said could only apply to the movements of one person."

"Would either of you kindly let me know who the hell you're talking about?" Ben appeared to have missed something.

Matt just looked at Carter and smiled. Marshall eyed Matt with a wink and then said to Ben, "Constable, assuming one of the missing persons in this case is the critter we've been attempting to identify, from what you've learned of them which, do you suppose, is the most likely suspect?"

Steel paused for a few seconds and then said, "The only person that jumps out at me is Simon McGivney."

Marshall asked, "Why Simon?"

"Well, for openers we know he's had experience with an Arctic Warfare Super Magnum that nearly killed Matt and yours truly."

"And what else?"

Reluctantly Ben said, "Okay I'll say it. McGivney matches what Matt said about Agatha Christie's *Ten Little Indians* tale."

"Oh, he's told that yarn to you too. It seems to be a favorite of Matt's. However, in this case I daresay it is a valid conjecture. Although both points are well taken, I'd rather pick McGivney as my second choice."

"So would I," Ames agreed.

Somewhat frustrated Steel said, "Well then, who do you guys think it is?"

"Good question," Matt said, attempting not to smile.

"A very good question," Marshall agreed without batting an eye. He then yawned and facetiously said, "I believe I'm experiencing a severe case of jet lag. What do you say, gentlemen, we call it a night. Oh yes, after breakfast we'll have to work up a plan that will fit in with a memorial service the community is planning for the recently deceased whirlybird victims; which reminds me, I have to call Sergeant Mahoney before sleep befalls me."

Before closing the door behind him Carter said, "Good night, gentlemen, may the force be with you."

Ames patted Ben on the back and said, "We're just pulling your chain, partner. We better get some sleep. Tomorrow promises to be a big day."

"Seriously, Matt, who is it you and Marshall suspect to be the serial killer? Really, I have to know."

"Ask yourself, Constable Steel, who among the missing persons would most likely pull a rabat out of a hat, and I don't mean the kind that jumps around on all fours?"

CHAPTER 38

Sentiments of Closure

Tracey Hamilton sat at a writing table in the apartment directly across the hall from Matt and Ben; Carter's was next to theirs. She'd been thinking of her grandmother's unfinished poem, *Longships Lighthouse*. While contemplating recent events, alone and moved to tears, Tracey accepted that the woman she loved with all her heart had gone to be a better place.

Wiping away the moisture from her face, Tracey placed the pen she'd been using in its holder and picked up the note she addressed to Matt. The handsome woman then turned her gaze toward the window that embraced an awe-inspiring panoramic view of Lands End western shores. Ms. Hamilton realized that if her nana's poem were to be completed, as Jessica indicated she intended to do, Tracey believed she needed to visit Longships lighthouse for the inspiration necessary to compose her grandmother's final stanza. Perhaps the gesture might bring proper closure to what a dedicated grand-daughter was feeling. She didn't know. Maybe too it would be a fitting tribute to Jessica's students. Again, Tracey was unsure. Without further deliberation, before anyone appeared to be awake and moving about, Hamilton gathered up her shoulder bag and set out to accomplish that which might at least bring a sigh of relief to the remorse she was feeling for her grandmother.

As they crossed paths in the hotel corridor on their way to breakfast, Marshall asked Ames to ascertain from Coroner Quinton one or two notable achievements Hayes and Latham may have merited in recent years. "I don't relish the idea standing at the podium with both hands in my pockets with nothing to say when I'm supposed to be eulogizing two dead citizens I hardly knew. Right now, until he's brought to justice, I'm up to my teeth with this mind-boggling maniac."

"Okay, Chief, Ben and I will attend to it after we eat. You go ahead. I'll see if Tracey is available to join us in the dining room."

Steel, as he exited his and Matt's suite, noticed Ames in the corridor. He said, "This note was left under our door. It's for you. Your name is on it."

"I'd better get my act together. I had to have walked right by it when I left the room before you."

"Negative, you stepped *on* it; unless this heel print belongs to someone else."

Ignoring his partner, Ames read the missive. He appeared concerned.

Ben asked, "Is anything wrong, Matt?"

"Tracey's on her way to Longships lighthouse. She wants to finish writing her grandmother's poem there. For all we know our phantom killer may have decided to make his presence felt where we would least expect him to be. We'd better see to her safety without delay."

Marshall was immediately informed of the latest turn of events. It was then his cellphone beeped. After listening to the brief message, he disconnected. "That was Sergeant Mahoney of homicide. Melanie Belldonger was found stabbed to death at Victoria Station. Crime scene detectives are presently documenting her personal effects. Forget Quinton. I'll think of something. You two locate that girl of yours, Matt. In the meantime I'll hurry up headquarters for reinforcements."

CHAPTER 39

Startling Revelations

It didn't take long for Marshall Carter to confirm his suspicions about the exclusive Coventry Gardens serial killer's identity. A startling revelation was staring the Superintendent of Scotland Yard in the face the moment he opened the email dispatch from Sergeant Mahoney. Although the transcript before him could not be deemed conclusive evidence, Melanie Belldonger's diary (illuminating her well-kept secret dated entries) coincided with the exact movements of Cameron Vogel, a patient she nursed at the Monroe Psychiatric Institute shortly after the war in Iraq ended.

Among the aliases he used, there was a solitary name that incriminated an individual associated with the case. The serial killer, in carrying on his notorious escapades while pretending to be an upstanding member of an obscure English hamlet famous for its tourist attractions, was identified as a wanton murderer in a hand written descriptive account by his former lover who had become his latest victim.

Superintendent Carter believed that Cameron Vogel concocted a pseudonym for his unique disguise after terminating the life of one of a cruise ship's passengers returning to England, as Belldonger asserted in an excerpt of her diary. She didn't want to believe it, but it was odd that Cameron's costume on the evening of the Masquerade Ball mimicked the bloke's profession who had been reported missing when the ocean liner from Sri Lanka docked at Bristol. It hadn't dawned on Melanie at the time, but she began to have second thoughts about what might have occurred when she later learned that the person who somehow ended up dead in the sea was the donor of Vogel's *party regalia*. Although the diary entry was brief, there was enough inference in it to confirm what Carter already suspected.

Melanie's second revelation gave Marshall Carter grave concern. Now that he learned Reed Latham and Sheriff Hayes had been in cahoots with Melanie Belldonger in pillaging the community for several years, particularly during the height of the tourist season- how was he to justify words of eloquence in his speech, when, in fact; the two blatant criminals he'd been asked to commend were nothing more than common thieves?

Ames and Steel were both relieved to see Tracey Hamilton sitting quietly by the wharf gazing at the turbulent sea in the distance. Since its reinforced construction in 1875, Longships lighthouse appeared to be repelling the onslaught of crashing waves, as though their mighty thrusts lacked significant force to upend the majestic tower. The base of the monolith could not be visibly discerned, and yet the strength and resistance of its structure reiterated the precise description Jessica O'Brien gave to the mighty monument she so eloquently portrayed from a poet's point view: sturdy, unshaken, standing strong, towering and unrelenting.

Turning her head toward the two detectives as they approached her, Tracey said, "I wouldn't be surprised if Nana were sitting right here when she wrote the first stanza of her poem."

"Let it rest, darling. For all we know Mrs. O'Brien and all the other missing persons are alive and well."

"Thanks, Matt, I wish it were only true. This may sound silly, but I was just now thinking of all the countless people who died in all the senseless wars going back to the ancient civilizations. If even a portion of them could have lived a full life, how many more gifted artists there would have been. When will we ever learn that the killing must stop?"

The tears finally came. They flowed freely. "I can't help it Matt. Nana is dead. I know she is. It's not that she's gone that hurts so much, but how she must have died. It had to have been horrible for her. Honestly, Matt, you must catch this monster. He has no regard for human dignity, nor does he have the license to take it upon himself to cut short that which only God can give and rightfully take away."

Lifting Tracey from her seated position, Ames held her close. "Dearest," his voice was tender and caring, "everything you said is true, every word of it. I wish I knew what to say right now, and even if I did, I can't imagine it would make much sense at all. However, darling, this I do know. You and I, in the manner by which we live our lives, must be the *beacon of hope* Jessica was referring to in her poem. Your nana's reference to Longships lighthouse as a *watchtower of might* should be a constant reminder to those who read her verse that we all should conduct our lives in truth, knowing full well that everyone is truly a reflection of God's love."

Removing a tissue from her pocket, Tracey wiped away a few lingering tears. "Thanks, Matt," she said, "all I can say right now is that you and Nana would have gotten along famously."

Ben felt the need to say, "Tracey, like Matt said, there's still a chance that Mrs. O'Brien is still with us."

"It's not that I've given up hope, Ben. You might say I'm currently in the process of conjuring up the nerve to accept the fact God may have already decided to take Jessica to that wonderful place she so often asserted could never be adequately explained away in any language."

Brandt Moore's train pulled into Penzance Station. He then rented a room at Kelly's Bed and Breakfast. Despite the hype going on pertaining to the recent copter crash, he'd been oblivious to it all. Moore was deep in thought with other urgent business; something about preparing a special package that would topple down a 220-year-old west coast British monument with three Scotland Yard detectives entrapped inside and nowhere to go.

CHAPTER 40

Pressing Forward

Whatever the reason for its dysfunction a maladjusted brain, upon deciphering messages it receives from a distorted mind- invariably transmits its lethal signals into destructive action. Amazingly, Cameron Vogel's malignant thought processes remained dormant during such times he received the best healthcare and professional assistance. However, years had passed before his psychological behavior suddenly turned sour. The voices, as he so called them, spontaneously flared from within and reclaimed their control over Vogel's schizophrenic, weaker self. Remarkably, it had been Melanie Belldonger's rehabilitative techniques that had kept Cameron's killer instincts from resurfacing much sooner.

For Vogel to get close to the three detectives without raising a red flag he needed to engineer a new identity. An afternoon newspaper had been left by Cameron's door, compliments of the house. The headline read:

Lands End Copter Crash Still
Under Investigation

After reading about the incident, Vogel felt no remorse for either of the deceased. Everyone connected to his insanity at the time he murdered a clergyman on the Bristol cruise ship dissolved into a blur, including the Coventry Gardens victims he stashed away in a common tomb to commemorate his madness. First and foremost, however, according to Cameron Vogel's latest imaginings, the three Scotland Yard detectives were next on his list to die. It was essential, according to the nagging voices, that this occurrence should take place soon, very soon.

Superintendent Carter in all likelihood would return to Scotland Yard at his earliest convenience. Vogel had to act swiftly. Glancing out from behind the curtain of his second floor guest room, his eyes focused on a passer-by ambling across Queens Square. The lantern in the pedestrian's hand gave Cameron an idea for the perfect scenario that would place his unsuspecting victims just where he wanted them to be. It would also give him the opportunity to visit Parson Wingate's old hunting ground.

CHAPTER 41

Carter's Briefing

By the time Ames and Steel returned to the office Superintendent Carter had already prepared coffee and doughnuts for them. Matt explained to his boss that because of the turbulent sea Tracey Hamilton never made it to the lighthouse. However, he did feel that the time she spent gazing at her grandmother's *beacon of hope* helped Tracey to be more accepting to the things she could not alter, and that in the final analysis surrender to God's will was first and foremost in all the things she needed to bear.

"I like that woman's attitude." Then with a quaint smile Marshall added, "Matt, I'm beginning to believe there's something between you two."

"Thanks, Marshall; for once in your life I think you're on to something."

Carter, having more important things to discuss, did not wish to continue bantering. "Gentlemen," he said, "have a seat. While you two were at Lands End, I've been in contact with headquarters. In regard to the late Mrs. Belldonger- whose brief marriage to a Sergeant Harrison Belldonger of the Naval reserves lasted for the space of two weeks (his sub was torpedoed in the Persian Gulf) Scotland Yard has recovered from her body a personal diary that paints a much clearer picture as to what we're up against.

"To begin with, it has been confirmed Nathaniel Wingate's finger prints were the only ones on our list of suspects which could not be identified in the data base under that name. However, whoever it was that killed Melanie Belldonger left plenty of hands-on evidence at the scene of the crime. An unequivocal match of thumb impressions has been substantiated. Forensics validates they belong to Cameron Vogel and, from what Melanie said in her diary, he and Parson Wingate are one and the same.

"According to what she had written, Melanie was Vogel's nurse, lover, and soul mate ever since their paths crossed in the Monroe Sanatorium. Furthermore, Mrs. Belldonger has been his unwitting accomplice from the moment she helped him escape from the asylum. She says here." Carter proceeded to read from a printed e-mail page of her diary; "*Melanie,* apparently that's what she named her personal memoir, *I daresay, it was Cameron who threw that missing clergyman overboard. You know it's true. Don't you recall; it happened soon before the Bristol cruise ship reached port? He must have found out that the bloke had been a last minute replacement at the Coventry Gardens vicarage- and assumed his position under a different name, Parson Nathaniel Wingate. It's just like 'im. My precious luv could convince the queen herself that he indeed was the king and whoever she'd been married to all this time was an imposter.*"

It took Marshall most of the morning to review the salient passages of Melanie Belldonger's diary with his two detectives. In documenting the tourist embezzlement configuration Melanie incriminated Sheriff Hayes and Shire Latham in the three-way pilfering affair. It was then Ames and Steel were able to piece together much of what previously blurred their vision earlier. From the get-go Sheriff Hayes never appealed to either of them as a true representative of the law enforcement profession they held in such high esteem. No wonder he maintained his position all these years. Shire Latham had been the brains of the disdainful outfit, but it was Rupert whose lawful credentials enabled the clandestine trio to move about their shady enterprise without being conspicuous while accomplishing their nefarious deeds.

Reed Latham never expressed a genuine concern for any of the missing persons in his shire. At such times several citizens were unexplainably disappearing he insisted that the tourist season could not be compromised. His ignoring the problem was inexcusable to say the least; but who was to know the esteemed public official's primary focus was engaged in pillaging the community he had sworn to uphold?

Simply speaking the three embezzlers sold counterfeit lottery tickets whose grand prizes were programmed to be won by fictitious tourists. Occasionally a local from the township made a lot of noise when his or her straw was drawn, but it would always be for a far lesser aggregate than what the other top amounts yielded. Since the inception of their corrupt scheme, the bandits had accumulated an absorbent amount of pound notes. Melanie, in reference to yet another passage in her diary, indicated that Shire Latham had set up promotional lottery booths wherever tourists flocked to highlighted tour guide attractions.

In characterizing Wingate, Carter explained that Vogel had chosen the perfect cover for the ill-will wreaked while impersonating a man of the cloth. However difficult to imagine, it was his recessive Jekyll personality that protected Cameron's dominant Hyde escapades. The parson's falsely documented papers, charismatic charm, and former nurse's unswerving devotion enabled him to plan and execute his every deceptive ploy. Carter also believed, as did his associates, that a heap of bodies were buried close by; but where they could be still remained an unnerving puzzlement that needed to be promptly addressed.

It was then Marshall picked up the phone and called Scotland Yard. "Mahoney, how many troops have you been able to muster up?" Pause, "We're going to need more than that." Pause. "I don't care. Send the janitor, if you have to." Pause. "An East End London Girl; and she speaks Cockney? Perfect. Send her. And Mahoney, I want the backups to arrive in less than two hours." Pause. "That's for you to figure out." Click.

Carter just looked at his two detectives who remained silent and said, "Any comments, gentlemen?"

Ames casually declared, "No, but do you really think it would make a hell-of-a difference if Mahoney showed up with a hundred agents?"

Be as it may, Patrick Mabry was already in the process of making his next move, and Tracey Hamilton was very much a part of it.

CHAPTER 42

Note of Deception

Tracey Hamilton was not a total stranger to Cameron Vogel. Shortly after the imposter exercised his bold audacity in assuming the identity of Parson Nathaniel Wingate, she had been introduced to him while visiting her grandmother who had taken a liking to the new minister. Amazingly, it was his inaugural awe-inspiring sermon which he delivered with such charm and eloquence to the Episcopal community that dispelled anyone's inkling to question his credentials. As it were, the parishioners overwhelmingly accepted the dynamic unknown preacher with open arms and wholeheartedly welcomed him to spearhead their humble congregation.

Vogel's latest disguise blended perfectly with its surroundings. Camouflaged in make-up to distort his recognizable features, he donned an outfit that took on the appearance of a run-of-the-mill lighthouse keeper. In connection to the enormous stash of money he found in Melanie's carrying case, Cameron did not waste precious time pondering how she got it. However, the ready cash did speed up the process in providing everything he needed to complete whatever preparations were necessary to raise the final curtain of his Coventry Gardens malicious killing spree.

While in the midst of devising his plan of destruction, Vogel spied Mrs. O'Brien's niece entering the Pendleton Hotel. He immediately assumed she must have been in close contact with the Scotland Yard detectives he'd been compelled by his compulsive nagging voices to eradicate. Following her into the lounge he caught a glimpse of Tracey striding up the garish, red carpeted staircase. Not wishing to be conspicuous, the serial killer swaggered over to the registration desk and told the clerk he'd like to have a single room for the night.

"Sign here, please, he said, "That will be thirty pounds in advance. Breakfast is served from six to nine. Oh yes, I also need to see your credentials with a photo I.D."

"I must have left them in the motorcar with my luggage. I'll tend do it, after I register." Before returning the ledger to the clerk who'd been distracted by a third party, Cameron flipped back a page and noticed that Tracey Hamilton had recently procured state room 212.

Vogel then quickly left the hotel, hopped in his mini and went directly to Macintyre's Rent-a-Craft shipyard. After placing a deposit on a seventeen foot bow rider runabout, he asked that it be taken to the Lands End Marina where he'd be taking it out for a brief fishing jaunt within the hour, and that the bill should be made out in cash to Patrick Mabry.

Next, he purchased a small box of stationery at a nearby convenience store. Taking a few minutes to write two brief notes, Cameron addressed one to Tracey Hamilton and the other to Superintendent Carter of Scotland Yard. He then checked the boot of his mini rent-a-car that contained a satchel of explosives which would make it impossible to identify the remains of anyone experiencing its lethal discharge within a fifteen meter radius. To his satisfaction, it had not been tampered with by any curious seekers.

Checking his watch, Vogel reckoned that everything was going smoothly and in a timely manner. At last, the moment of truth had come. The final showdown was about to commence. He only hoped that Tracey Hamilton would be alone when he delivered to her the memo he scribbled in Marshall Carter's name. Of course! She loved her grandmother. Why wouldn't the lass respond in the manner he anticipated she would? Without further deliberation Cameron Vogel, a.k.a. Osgood Townsend, a.k.a. Parson Nathaniel Wingate, a.k.a.

Brandt Moore, a.k.a. Patrick Mabry, headed straight back to the Pendleton Hotel.

Luck had been with the serial killer. Thinking it was Matt Ames who knocked on her door, Tracey opened it quickly. Surprised to see a bearded stranger standing before her, she took a step backward.

"Didn't mean to alarm you Miss Tracey, you are Miss Tracey Hamilton?"

Composing herself, she answered with, "Yes, is there something I can do for you?"

It was then Vogel handed her the envelope which had Hamilton's name on it and said, "I was asked to give this to you and wait for a reply."

Upon tearing the seal away Hamilton read the letter. It stated:

Dear Tracey, Mrs. O'Brien and all the missing person have been located. She's been asking for you. Matt, Ben, and I are with the paramedics now. The courier of this message will take you to our present location. Watch for the flashing lights. Come quickly. M. Carter

In a panic Hamilton grabbed her jacket and, while still clutching the note tightly in her hand, ushered the bearer of good tidings out of the room. With tears in her eyes Tracey had neither the foggiest notion as to where she was going nor the faintest idea who it was taking her there.

CHAPTER 43

Open Discussion

"Gentlemen, it really doesn't matter how many agents Mahoney is able to recruit. The point is we must take the offensive. Up until now Cameron Vogel's been calling all the shots, and the climax of his cleverly orchestrated murderous orgy is soon to be realized."

"Don't expect a disagreement from either of us, Marshall; Ben and I have done everything humanly possible to anticipate his every ensuing move. Cameron Vogel's insane behavior is the most bizarre case the Yard has had to deal with since Jack the Ripper. As we speak, he's undoubtedly readying himself to serve the three of us up for a late afternoon snack; and that's precisely why you've been in constant communication with Mahoney.

"From what he's intimated in two of his dossiers, that we're on his hit list, and the graphic account Melanie Belldonger portrayed of Vogel in her diary, Cameron's poised to rid the world of our carcasses and has already designated the time and place. I suspect our unsavory friend is fixing to carry out the finale of his subtle scheme with sounding drums and clashing symbols sometime during your eulogy speech this afternoon."

"Matt, you don't have to remind me. What you said is true. I'm counting on Scotland Yard reinforcements to prevent that from happening. In any event, gentlemen, we've been sworn to uphold the law and have no other recourse than to remain steadfast to our solemn duty."

Nodding in agreement Constable Steel said, "I've been giving the matter considerable thought. We mustn't forget Vogel is a casualty of war. In cross-checking his M.O. it's quite obvious that Cameron's irrational behavior coincides with the type of mental aberration that's caused by certain nerve gases he had been vulnerable to while serving in the Iraqi campaign.

"I daresay his probable exposure to Agent Orange would indisputably account for the poor bloke's irresponsible actions. It's safe to assume the effects of war has turned Vogel into a ticking time bomb that releases lethal tension whenever the pressure or whatever it is inside his tormented skull prompts him to kill. Melanie Belldonger tried to find a way to get through to him, but despite her efforts, she couldn't rearrange the blighted pieces of his mind to perceive things rationally; no one can."

"Of course!" Carter's voice resounded with a hint of excitement. "Why else would he kill the one person in the world that smothered him with care and affection? At the time he crossed paths with Melanie at Victoria Station his Hyde personality must have discerned her as an immediate threat. Vogel's pressure cooker, so to speak, boiled over and; unable to connect the dots, he killed her. Well, you know what I mean."

Inspector Ames added, "Marshall, what you said kind of explains why he did away with the likes of Jessica O'Brien. She'd be the last human being anyone would want to harm. The elderly nature loving victim was easy prey for Vogel who, in the guise of Parson Nathaniel Wingate, acted upon his demonic fetish at a time he was unable to control his evil inhibitions.

"It's a consensus of opinion among the three of us that Cameron has two distinct personalities. The dominant one has taken on the demeanor of a psychopathic killer that has usurped complete dominion over his recessive, weaker counterpart. It's clearly evident that Vogel's plight can be paralleled to Stevenson's Dr. Jekyll. When Cameron's uncontrollable urges peak, his dominant (homicidal) psyche manifests itself, as did Mr. Hyde at which times he tyrannized Dr. Jekyll. In Cameron Vogel's case the paralysis of war has grossly created a monster within which periodically renders the poor bloke helpless. Whatever the fear that incites his Hyde disposition to emerge, it invariably results in deviant acts of homicide."

Both Steel and Carter acknowledged Ames's remarks with a vigorous affirmative "Here, here!"

Marshall then stood up and said, "Gentlemen, I believe we've come a long way in attempting to make sense of this case. However, let's first have something to eat. Then we'll try to figure out what Vogel has in his sick mind for this afternoon. At least our reinforcements will have arrived. Perhaps their presence may put a chink in his plans. Matt, why don't you ask Ms. Hamilton to join us for lunch? Tell her I insist."

As Mabry's mini sped towards Lands End, Tracey asked the driver where exactly her grandmother had been found and was she truly alright. He explained that all Superintendent Carter said was that her grandmother was okay, and the other two detectives urged Mabry not to tarry in delivering the dispatch to her, as he'd been so ordained to do.

Tracey momentarily wondered if she'd been hallucinating, experiencing a dream come true. As the auto approached the rental station adjacent to the marina, Hamilton looked around and in desperation started to say, "Superintendent Carter said in his message to watch for the flashing lights. Where are you taking me? Where's my na…"

Mabry snapped, "Look there toward the lighthouse!" The moment Tracey instinctively turned her head, the bottle of chloroform came out. Patrick then withdrew from his black denim jacket a serviette which he doused with the inhalant. Before the unsuspecting victim realized what was happening, the cloth, (bearing its potent anesthetic) was pressed against Hamilton's nose and mouth. She succumbed with hardly a struggle. Amazingly the entire action took place wherein the vehicle had still not come to a full stop. Again, luck was with Mabry.

While all this was occurring, the boat he procured earlier was being lowered into its slip.

The imposter showed his bogus identification to the wharf attendant and then returned to his conveyance where his unconscious prey lay back in her seat. Tracey's relaxed position gave anyone who may have noticed her the distinct impression she'd been napping. Making certain the coast was clear Patrick whisked Tracey Hamilton onto the boat. He then quickly backtracked to his car. Propping the note he'd written to Carter on the dashboard, Mabry checked the weather report. To his satisfaction it hadn't changed. While the motor idled, he rolled down the car windows and turned up the stereo. Upon retrieving the carefully packaged bomb from his Mini, Patrick Mabry swiftly returned to the launch and slowly motored toward Longships lighthouse where the choppy waters Tracey had gazed upon during the earlier part of the day had begun to pick up momentum.

Within minutes the rented craft neared the rocks surrounding the huge obelisk. Cool ocean air filled Tracey's lungs and revived her, just as Mabry had anticipated. Cautiously wedging his motor craft between two protruding boulders, he then assisted Hamilton to climb aboard Carn Bras, the largest of Longships bastion of rocks upon which the majestic tower stood. Retrieving a key from his waistcoat, Patrick pressed Tracey forward to climb a few steps before unlocking the lighthouse's lower storey portal.

Five minutes before Ames returned to the office Marshall Carter received Cameron Vogel's shocking note which had been delivered to him by a dock worker who had investigated the din made by the blaring music emanating from the Mini Coup. Benjamin Steel, having been preoccupied with his computer, had not been informed of its contents.

Upon entering the office, Matt said, "I can't understand it. When Tracey and I returned to the hotel, I could have sworn she said that all she wanted to do this morning was simply take a nap before having lunch."

Ben, attempting to be optimistic, said, "Perhaps she decided to go for a stroll. It's a perfectly gorgeous day, one would think."

It was then Carter interrupted the conversation with, "There's no easy way to explain to either of you what I've got to say. Matt, have a seat. This communiqué has just been delivered to me."

As Marshall Carter shared the contents of Vogel's note with Ames and Steel, the twin engine plane with reinforcements from London approached Lands End amphibian landing strip. Ten agents were aboard. Sergeant Mahoney was among them, and so was the detective who once lived in East London where she and Melanie Belldonger (then Melanie Brister) coincidentally grew up together.

CHAPTER 44

Wilma Barnhart

Matthew Ames responded to Marshall Carter's note scrawled by the fictitious pastor of a community who had been kept in the dark about their minister's venomous behavior, as he would react to a poison dart that penetrated the very depths of his heart. And while its contents sent bitter chills through Constable Steel as well, Carter had exhibited no emotion after reading it. He was like a resilient fortress. Although Marshall felt compassion for his field men's inner seethe of fury, it was his job to maintain self-control and to be resistant to evil threats; otherwise the very foundation of the law enforcement agency which he'd been privileged to command for twenty years would gradually begin to compromise its moral purpose, lose its effectiveness, and finally come crashing down like a house of cards, so he believed.

None-the-less, Cameron Vogel's memo did put to rest a mind-blogging question, the one connected with a query Steel and Ames entertained at the time a sniper's bullet sent them scampering down Longships lighthouse's wrought iron steps, something to do with what Ben wrote in his notepad about a foul odor the two couldn't quite diagnose. It was unconscionable. In which ever method he used to kill them, Vogel had been utilizing the unmanned tower as a crypt to stash his victims!

"Gentlemen, from what Melanie Belldonger had stated in her diary and this memo that I hold in my hand, we are able to confirm that there is a serial killer in our midst. However, since the community at the moment is not in harms way, for the exception of Ms. Tracey Hamilton whose situation is tenuous, we'll make no official statement pertaining to his existence. All accounts pertaining to Vogel's case history, his aliases, and the plight of any of his victims must stay under wraps until the current situation has been resolved.

"Benjamin, I want you to hightail it to the marina and, as soon as our reinforcements arrive, inform Sergeant Mahoney to commandeer however many vessels are necessary to coordinate a blockade around Longships lighthouse, lest our impetuous fugitive attempts to escape. Then tell him to bring that female agent from East London to me. After Matt and I procure an interior sketch of the lighthouse, it behooves us to take a gander at what that albatross out there looks like on the inside. We'll rendezvous at the pier and take it from there. I'd say forty-five minutes should do it. Enough said. Hop to it, constable, we can't afford to keep Ms. Hamilton in bondage any longer than necessary."

On his way out the door Steel paused and said to Carter, "Chief, do you think Tracey is still…"

"Alive? You heard Vogel's message. Quite frankly, although you cannot always believe the rantings of a serial killer, I'd say in this case his main objective is three Scotland Yard agents and not Ms. Hamilton. Cameron's just using her to make sure you, Matt, and me show up in one neat package, so as to finish us off in one fell swoop."

Glancing at his watch, Marshall said, "We haven't much time, but I've thought of something. Granted it's a long shot, but who knows, it just might work?" At that, Steel, given a capsule of assurance, bolted out the door.

"Thanks," Ames said to Carter. "I very much needed to hear what you just said."

Like clock work, everything seemed to gel as Marshall hoped it would. Ten reinforcements arrived and eight of them had already been poised by Carter to stand by for further instructions. Constable Steel,

Sergeant Mahoney, and the female detective were gathered at the pier's edge while Marshall discussed with Matt how the two would incorporate into a plan of action the scroll Ames cradled under his arm. After they completed their brief tête-á-tête, Sergeant Miles Mahoney formally introduced the lone woman recruit to the senior officers. "Gentlemen, this is Detective Wilma Barnhart. She transferred to homicide division from Traffic Control this morning. Wilma happened to be in the office, Marshall, at the time you phoned me to muster up whatever agents were available to help out here."

After everyone had been summarily acquainted, Carter said to Barnhart, "When Mahoney mentioned you were from the East Side, well, I had a purpose in mind for wanting you to be here."

"I gathered as much, from what Sergeant Miles told me. Before you ask, yes, I did know Melanie Brister. We grew up together. However, we parted ways when she opted to enlist in the army after becoming a nurse; I chose to serve in the navy. It wasn't until years later that I learned she'd married an army corporal, Hampton Belldonger, who tragically died when his sub blew up in the Persian Gulf. Poor lass, from what I understand, she never had a proper honeymoon."

Steel looked at Ames and said, "Matt, does Wilma's voice sound at all familiar?"

Ames remembered and said, *"When you hear the steeple bells ringing, you think of me."*

Superintendent Carter, seemingly ignoring Matt's response, turned to Mahoney and said, "After we're finished here, see to it that the captain of this police clipper has a portable bull horn that works."

"Police boats usually do," Mahoney answered. Noticing a look of disapproval on his superintendent's face (for voicing his smart-ass quip in the presence of a woman) he apologetically added, "Yes, sir, my bad, I'll doubly check to see that it does."

"Gather around, people," Marshall's tone carried a sense of urgency, "I want everyone to listen up. If we're going to be successful in carrying out this mission, everyone must be on the same page and feel free to speak openly in offering any suggestions that may seem relevant. With that being said, I wish to read to you a communiqué I received this morning from a criminally insane, homicidal patient by the name of Cameron Vogel who had escaped several years ago from London's Monroe Sanatorium."

Carter then read the note he initially received from a dock worker who found it while investigating the din stemming from the scene of Mabry's mini. ***"Superintendent Carter, it was Tracey Hamilton who insisted that I bring her to Longships lighthouse. You see, she wanted very much to see her grandmother. Sadly to say, Tracey will be very disappointed when she finds it difficult to identify Mrs. O'Brien's remains in the heap of rotted flesh. Superintendent Carter, Inspector Ames, and Constable Steel, should you decide to exchange your lives for Mrs. Hamilton's, climb the outer tower steps and enter the lighthouse through the keeper's third storey emergency porthole. You'll find it unlatched and quite accessible. I forewarn you. For the woman's sake arrive by 3 p.m. Don't be late, and do not bring any extra guests; otherwise, Tracey dies amid the rocks below. The clock is ticking."***

Glancing at his watch Ames noted the team had fifty minutes to review his and Carter's plan to save Tracey's life, even if it meant others might die in her stead.

It was then Carter retrieved Melanie Belldonger's diary from his jacket, the one Sergeant Mahoney brought with him from London and said, "Wilma, if you wouldn't mind, I'd like you to read this passage before we proceed."

"I'd be delighted to, sir." Barnhart cleared her throat and began reading in her definitive natural dialect. *"I know if I don't move on, Cameron will one day kill me. I still love him dearly, I do. There has to be a cure. Melanie dear, you must confess. For all the terrible things he did, you know he's not to blame. As God is my witness, your luv's not truly responsible for what he did to all those poor innocent people he's done away with. T'was the voices in his head that gave him no peace of mind is what made him do it. I swear to it, those nasty voices made Cameron behave the way he did. I daresay whoever invented that what-cha-ma-call-it; methylphosphonothioate (nerve gas) should be hog-tied."*

After Wilma had finished speaking, Ames suddenly realized why his ingenious boss wanted her to partake in this mission. He even had remembered to have Mahoney send a 'To Whom It May Concern' dispatch that Superintendent Carter regrettably would not be able to attend this afternoon's eulogy service to be held in honor of the recent helicopter victims.

CHAPTER 45

Interior Analysis

Whatever the situation might have been at Longships lighthouse or whether in fact Tracey Hamilton was actually brought there by Cameron Vogel, the team needed to study the structure's basic component parts, including its various entry and exit points- if indeed a rescue attempt would have any chance of being successful. According to what had been said in the serial killer's note, Carter and the others believed the life threatening mission they were about to embark upon was not a hoax.

The core rescue team gathered in the stateroom of the coastguard surveillance cruiser docked at the pier in hopes of devising a feasible plan in freeing Ms. Hamilton from her loathsome oppressor. However, Carter, Ames, Steel, Mahoney, and Barnhart first had to pore over the conveyance document Marshall and Matt obtained from the local deeds office. It was then Ames unfurled a blueprint depicting an interior configuration of Longships lighthouse. Steel assisted his partner by firmly securing his end of the unraveled scroll to the oval table. Before giving a detailed analysis of the sketch Matt took a brief moment to make a personal statement.

"Let me begin by saying this. Superintendent Carter, Constable Steel and I are in total accord that Tracey Hamilton who's being held hostage in Longships lighthouse, regardless of the consequences, is our first and foremost priority."

"Inspector," it was Sergeant Barnhart that felt she needed to speak up. "I think you should know Sergeant Mahoney shares my sentiment as well. The two of us are fully committed to do whatever is necessary in bringing this assignment to a speedy and successful conclusion, whatever the cost."

Unable to suppress the proud look on his face Carter gave Matt a nod indicating to him that he should proceed.

Ames cleared his throat, pointed to the chart and said, "Longships tower is composed of three major storeys. This bottom section is where the water tanks and lighthouse supplies are kept. Sergeants Mahoney and Barnhart will enter the tower at this level. Notice the flight of open-ended curved steps that ascends to the second storey. It is absolutely necessary that neither of you are noticed by Vogel. To give himself assurance that we're not attempting to deceive him he expects Marshall, Ben, and me only."

Mahoney inquired, "Won't Vogel spy the two of us getting off the boat when we exit the craft?"

"There's a blind spot at the top of the lighthouse," Ames answered. "As you can see here, because of this structural overhang, Cameron will not have a vantage point of spotting anyone disembarking from the police boat."

Moving his index finger to the next level on the chart, Ames continued to engage Mahoney and Barnhart's attention. "There's a door at the top of these stairs that will enable you to gain entry here. This section is comprised of the absentee lighthouse keeper's living quarters. It includes a kitchenette, parlor, and food pantry. You'll then continue up the next curving flight of steps until you reach the base of the third storey which is where the light keeper's bedroom is located. Do not force your way through this door. If you cannot open it with a pass key, tap softly three times. Should that be the case, Marshall and I will have to devise a way to distract Vogel while Constable Steel opens the portal from our side. Under no circumstances can Cameron be led to believe that a woman officer is present among us.

"Now just above the third storey room is a small compartment where miscellaneous items are kept. I strongly suspect Vogel and Tracey will be held up in that loft. It's undoubtedly secure and quite impossible for us to be a threat to him from our precarious vulnerable position. Without having to say, Cameron will have some explosive device strapped to his chest, to remind us that he's in control and we're not."

Ben said, "Matt, there appears to be a helipad just above the wood and copper lantern. Wouldn't it be easier for us to enter the lighthouse from that vantage point?"

"Constable Steel," Carter commended, "You have a fine eye for details. However, the slightest inkling whereby Vogel believes he is being deceived could very well mean curtains for all of us . We mustn't forget Cameron Vogel is a psychopathic killer. He's likely to regard anything we might do that does not conform to his specific instructions an act of aggression."

"Anything else," Ames asked?

Carter said, "Thank you Matt, I'll take it from here." Turning to Sergeants Mahoney and Barnhart, Marshall continued to say, "It is my unpleasant duty to remind the two of you what you are apt to expect while forging your way to the third storey chamber. There's no way of determining the method of how Cameron Vogel disposed of his victims or what he might have even done with them. However, his last communiqué is a strong indication that all the Coventry Gardens missing persons are gathered in a heap somewhere in the lighthouse.

"In any case, it is critical that you both attain your positions at the entranceway to the third level as quickly as possible. Mahoney, disregard anything and everything you see. You must tightly trail Sergeant Barnhart up the lighthouse steps. If, by chance, Wilma should misstep during the ascent, it is your responsibility to prevent her from going over the side. And, should *you* falter, for Tracey's sake, make certain you have the presence of mind to leave the bull horn behind."

"Say what?" At the ensuing burst of laughter, Sergeant Mahoney's disconnect to what his boss had just said became apparent. Whenever a release of tension was needed Superintendent Marshall Carter always seemed to find a way to provide it.

CHAPTER 46

Prelude to the Finale - Part I

Although it was apparent that Cameron Vogel intended to blow up the lighthouse with everyone in it, Superintendent Carter had the tower strategically surrounded by reinforcements before his police launch arrived at Carn Bras. All personnel had been ordered to stay out of visual sight lest Cameron decided to take pop shots at them with his AWSM, which he undoubtedly kept close at hand.

Whatever plans the serial killer might have anticipated for making an escape, Marshall made sure that would not happen. Carter, from the moment he read the letter delivered to him at the office a few hours ago, did have a gut feeling all was not hopelessly lost. The fact that Vogel offered to make an exchange for Tracey Hamilton's life signified the distinct possibility Cameron may be open to entertain other options. In any case the team needed to follow Marshall's instructions to the letter.

When the launch reached its destination Ames, Carter, and Steel bolted from the boat, crossed over to the exterior ladder, and commenced their ascent. It wasn't until they reached the second storey level that Sergeants Mahoney and Barnhart scrambled to the ground entrance at the near side of the tower. The latch key would not turn in the lock. Marshall had warned them beforehand that Vogel, in the event a workman needed to gain entry, might have changed the mechanism. Miles withdrew his pistol, attached a silencer to it, and fired one round at his target. In a moment's time both officers with their torches ablaze were safely inside the majestic lighthouse.

Nothing appeared out of the ordinary. There were certainly no dead bodies lying about. However, a foul, pungent odor prompted the two officers to cover their faces with surgical masks they had brought with them. The beam of their flashlight quickly found the curving staircase that led to the second level. Mahoney, recalling Carter taking Sergeant Barnhart aside for a few minutes before they left the pier, said in a soft voice, "If it's not too personal to ask, what does the diary Carter gave to you, or this megaphone, have to do with anything?"

Wilma whispered back, "Marshall said that both these items may very well be considered a matter of life-and-death. So please, Sergeant Mahoney, keep that bull horn tightly in hand."

Reaching the second tier of the lighthouse, this time it was Sergeant Barnhart who applied the door key to its lock. Finding that it held secure the same procedure was used that unfastened the lower level entranceway. Upon entering the room, Wilma choked and nearly passed out at what she saw.

Cameron Vogel was true to his word. The rectangular portal entrance just above the second storey of the lighthouse was made accessible, just as he said it would be. Ames entered first, but when Marshall tried to squeeze through, Benjamin Steel had to assist him with a forceful nudge. Once the three were inside, Ames looked across the light keeper's bedroom. He could see the door Mahoney and Barnhart would secretly enter. Matt lifted his eyes in hopes of spying Tracey. She wasn't anywhere to be seen. He then quietly said to Carter, "Tracey and Vogel must be cradled in that niche below the copper lantern. Shouldn't we let them know we're here?"

Before Marshall responded a penetrating voice broke the silence. "The three of you remain where you are. Ms. Hamilton, I assure you, has not been harmed. She can hear, and she can see, but for the time being, she is not in a position to speak."

Abruptly changing the subject Vogel said, "Superintendent Carter, hats off! I wasn't truly certain you would show up. You and your subordinates are to be congratulated for offering yourselves as human sacrifices. Naturally, you're fully aware that everyone alive in this earthly tomb will soon be dead, excepting for me and perhaps Ms. Hamilton, if she can make her way safely down all those blighted steps before the explosives are discharged. Don't think for a moment the fleet of boats surrounding Longships lighthouse will prevent me from eluding your foolhardy scheme of ensnarement. Perhaps, before you die, I will enlighten you of the one thing you overlooked that will ensure my inevitable escape."

"Pardon me for the interruption. This is Superintendent Marshall Carter of Scotland Yard speaking. I'm assuming that I am addressing Cameron Vogel, a former detainee of the Monroe Psychiatric Center in London, and that Ms. Tracey Hamilton, as you have previously indicated, has not been harmed. Furthermore, I'm also assuming that you intend to give Ms. Hamilton sufficient time to leave this god-forsaken place under Constable Steel's escort, to be taken back to the mainland by the Border Patrol cruise ship that brought us here. I've already instructed the captain to sound three siren blasts the moment Ms. Hamilton has reached Lands End safely."

Vogel replied, "Superintendent Carter, I needn't have to remind you who is in charge here. However, since you asked, yes, I am Cameron Vogel. Shame on you, it certainly took Scotland Yard long enough to finally discover that I was the needle in the haystack you've been searching for all this time. Under the circumstances it was quite necessary; you understand, for me to have had to use various pseudonyms these past few weeks."

Somewhat perturbed with Marshall's arrogance, Vogel quickly added, "In reference to what you said regarding Ms. Hamilton, it is totally non-negotiable. She is quite capable exiting the lighthouse of her own accord. Should any of you make an attempt to intervene on her behalf, you have my word on it; she will be the first to die."

By now Cameron was fuming. His next ranting, filled with ire, caromed off the cylindrical walls with a resounding echo. "You've decided that Constable Steel will escort Ms. Hamilton! You've instructed the captain to sound three siren blasts! Superintendent Carter, might I remind you this is my domain, and that you have no jurisdiction here?!"

From the side of his mouth Marshall said to the others, "This lunatic's got more bats in his belfry than China has tea; he just self-appointed himself a judge."

C H A P T E R   4 7

Prelude to the Finale - Part II

Upon turning her eyes from the grim spectacle of rotting appendages that conveyed a macabre display of horror, Mahoney steadied Wilma in his arms. A rancid bed cover lay carelessly strewn over what appeared to be several mutilated corpses heaped in a pile. Embellishing the ghastliness, numerous decomposed rats reposed among the cadavers. Miles surmised that bromethalin, a rodenticide, or some other deadly poison had taken its toll on the four-legged scavengers that had been lured into the gruesome mortuary by the presence of decaying flesh.

Visibly distraught Sergeant Barnhart composed herself. She said, "I'll be alright, Miles; never in my life, those poor souls, how awful!"

Sensing the same bitter remorse his partner evinced, in response to what the two police officers had just encountered, Mahoney's subdued voice uttered, "We better move on, Wilma, the others are depending on us."

Approaching the flight of steps leading to the third storey portal, Sergeant Barnhart paused and said, "Mahoney, you need to go back and get the bull horn you dropped just as I swooned. I'd go myself, but I can't; I just can't."

Amid the aura of Longships crime scene Carter endeavored to imagine how Vogel intended to escape. The lighthouse was completely cordoned off by Scotland Yard detectives and Coastguard Reserves who responded to the emergency stress call initiated by Lands End Port Authority. Cameron couldn't possibly circumvent his situation by sea, so what else had he in mind?

Marshall's thoughts were interrupted by Matthew Ames's tirade when he suddenly became unglued. "Vogel," he shouted, "this is Chief Inspector Ames, I want to talk to Tracey Hamilton. If you don't produce her in five seconds, I'm going to climb up there and tear you to pieces."

Cameron, having calmed down a bit, said, "Do not threaten me, Inspector Ames. My AWSM, the one with which I could have killed you- this very moment is pointing at Constable Steel."

It was then Marshall Carter intervened. "Cameron," he said, "You need to have a little more patience with Inspector Ames. You see he's kind of stuck on Ms. Hamilton. Have a heart and cut him some slack. All he wants right now is a few last words with his sweetheart before we make the trade according to the terms you stipulated in your memo." Pausing, he added, "That is, unless you decide to call the whole thing off and come quietly with us to headquarters."

In reply to Marshall's quip Vogel said, "Superintendent Carter, you do have a disdainful sense of humor. Let's not have any more of it. However, being the three of you are about to breathe your last, I will allow Inspector Ames to have his brief tête-á-tête with Ms. Hamilton."

"Mr. Vogel," Constable Steel broke his silence, "It's difficult to see Tracey from this cramped area. Would it be okay for us to move to where we can better see her?"

Vogel pointed his torchlight toward the west side of the tower. He said, "The slightest sign of a weapon of any kind will spell *death* for the lady. Lift your hands high, all of you, and slowly follow the beam of my torch-light. Pause by the lamp stand and look up. I've already untethered Ms. Hamilton's wraps. Inspector Ames, you may converse with her for three minutes. We'll then negotiate matters before you die."

"Good show, Benjamin," Carter whispered as a spark of hope enlivened his spirit. The three would now be in position to shield Sergeant Barnhart.

The Scotland Yard detectives complied with Vogel's explicit instructions. They gingerly moved toward the third storey entranceway which connected to the living quarters below it. Next to a dust laden sofa by the door a vertical lamp stand emitted speckles of dim light from its moth eaten shade. Crossing his fingers Carter said a prayer that Sergeants Mahoney and Barnhart had reached their destination.

As Tracey moved out of the shadows into plain sight, Matt exhaled a breath of relief. No explosives had been attached to any part of her body that he could see. His voice tended to be calm and endearing. "Tracey dearest, are you alright?"

"No darling I'm not alright." Her words conveyed heartfelt fear and anger. "Nana's dead," she said, "and so are the others. You shouldn't have come, Matt. It's all so horrible." Turning her head toward Vogel, she boldly admonished him, "How could you have done such a thing? What did my grandmother or any of the others ever do to you?" Downtrodden and exhausted Tracey lifted her hands to her face and wept what few tears still remained within her.

"Darling," Ames was beside himself, "Don't say anything more. Try to take hold of yourself, dearest. Be brave, sweetheart. Cameron will keep his promise. I know he will. Tracey, for my sake, do whatever he tells you. It won't be long before you'll be free from all this. I love you, my darling. Be strong."

"Very touching, what a nice couple you two would have made." Cameron Vogel's sarcastic remark did not warrant a response.

Ever so gently, from the other side of the portal, Sergeant Barnhart inserted her key into the lock of the third storey tower door. Upon turning it she wondered if the tumbler would release the bolt.

CHAPTER 48

The Finale

C lick! It worked. Turning the knob, Sergeant Barnhart pushed the door open ever so slightly. Carter's heart skipped a beat. *They made it,* he thought to himself. While Vogel diverted his attention to secure Tracey's bonds, Marshall, Matt, and Ben cautiously inched closer to the door to serve as a protective shield for Wilma who had successfully wormed her way inside the room. Remaining in her crouched posture, Sergeant Barnhart turned the megaphone to the 'on' position. Realizing there had not been sufficient illumination to read the selected passages from Melanie Belldonger's diary, as previously planned in the scheme conjured up by Marshall Carter to deceive Cameron Vogel, she gulped.

At his vantage point beneath the lighthouse helipad Cameron noticed shrouds of gray mist gathering overheard. As expected the approach of the weather bureau's predicted forecast of a warm moist air mass began its decent over the cool ocean waters. It was the diminishing visibility blanketing the coastline that instigated a sudden rush of exhilaration which prompted Vogel's elated outburst.

"Gentlemen, it is finished." Cameron appeared to be hallucinating. "The final hour has come. Longships lighthouse shall no longer be a guiding torch for seafarers. Her transformation into smattering specks of brick and mortar will immortalize this historic occasion as a day of mindless infamy."

Ames shouted back. "Vogel, we made a bargain. I demand that you release Ms. Hamilton before you carry on what you intend to do with us."

"My humble apologies, Inspector Ames, you see circumstances have changed." To Tracey he said, "It's a pity I cannot take you with me, Ms. Hamilton. Though the sentiment may not be mutual, difficult as it may seem, I've rather grown quite fond you."

Sergeant Wilma Barnhart realized her discourse with Cameron Vogel had to captivate his imagination. She needed to convince him that it was Melanie Belldonger speaking- not an imposter. Furthermore, to intensify the distraction, she sensed it was all-important to interrupt him with a resounding reproach while he was still in the midst of prattling.

Carter, attempting to keep the despot preoccupied in hopes that Wilma would soon find an opportune moment to break into the conversation called out, "Vogel, I figured out how you plan to escape."

"You disappoint me, Superintendent Carter. Swallow your pride and admit to your ineptness. From the onset you and your amateur detectives have been scurrying around in circles. Among other things, it doesn't take a rocket scientist to calculate the possibility of anyone escaping from here to the mainland via parasail. However, the concept is ingenious; don't you think? You must also concede to the fact that even the infamous Sherlock Holmes would not have tracked me down, had I not permitted him to do so."

Carter shot back. "Touché, you got me there, Cameron. I should have truly given the matter sufficient forethought. Of course, it's all becoming crystal clear just now. An acquaintance of yours, does the name Parson Nathaniel Wingate strike a note? No matter, we won't concern ourselves about him at the moment. Be as it may, he undoubtedly had a hand in fabricating the unimaginable scenario you so aptly devised and brought to the light of my attention. Your array of disguises has certainly fooled me."

Deliberately being rudely abrupt, Carter injected a delicate issue into the conversation. He intended to be flippant. "Incidentally, Mr.

Vogel, I realize you have a tight schedule, but I would really like to know what made you decide to throw Melanie Belldonger under the bus. I thought you two were palzy-walzy."

Vogel was outraged. He bellowed. "What do you know of our relationship? Leave Melanie out of thi…"

Before the infuriated despot could finish his sentence, for Wilma Barnhart, it was now or never. The entire lighthouse upper chamber reverberated with a resounding echo, *"Cameron, luv, shame on you. 'Leave me out of this,' is that what you were about to say?" Listen carefully; I haven't much time."*

Vogel, in recognizing what appeared to be the voice of his former lover, was taken aback. "Melanie, it can't be you. You're dead." Then, recoiling from his initial shock, he said, "Carter, you and the others will pay dearly for this insulting game of charades. I demand to know where that ludicrous voice is coming fr…"

Before Cameron's dominant personality regained full control Wilma hammered back. Her voice was intense and commanding. *"Be still and do not utter another word, you ungrateful wretch. For all I've been to you in the past, it appalls me that you continue to permit those despicable inner voices to dismiss me as though I were a mere figment of days gone by."*

Recalling to mind excerpts from Melanie Belldonger's diary, Wilma delivered her extemporaneous speech flawlessly. She slowed the tempo of her words and spoke in a mournful cadence.

"Cameron, you have never known me to lie. My sweet petty boo, yes, you doubting Thomas, you have left me no alternative than to break my intimate promise. Petty boo," Wilma's voice resonated with passion, *"there, I said it again. Why shouldn't the world know I loved you, a monster who beckons to beguiling voices?"*

It was then, in an attempt to stifle the haunt, Vogel clasped his hands to his ears and cried out in trepidation, "Stop! Melanie, you're dead. I killed you. No more!"

Ignoring his outburst Sergeant Barnhart carried on at fever pitch. She was clueless as to what impact her niggling words might have on the pressure gauge of this abnormality without a conscience, how he would react to them, what he'd do next. If she could only inveigle him to escape from the unbearable strain and anguish she'd been subjecting to his fraying nerves.

Wilma continued to lambaste her teetering combatant without restraint. ***"Cameron,"*** the echo of what appeared to be Melanie's voice, vibrated eerily, ***"Do no harm to the woman. I promise. Only then will I release you of my haunts. Petty Boo (the voices) pay them no heed. Leave the woman be. Go now, luv. Set yourself free. I promise. Never again will I haunt you. Quickly! Go! Go before it's too late. Go!***

Sparked by a sudden siege of embroilment, an inexplicable flurry of bewilderment, Vogel glared at Tracey Hamilton, turned, and rapidly climbed the short flight of steps that led to the helipad. Carter and the others were amazed and speechless. They noticed Cameron disengage a lever and exit through a small hatch. Removing his breastplate laden with dynamite, he tossed it with a mighty thrust into the churning waters below. Upon impact it exploded in a fury, creating a tremendous surge of sea water to blanket the lighthouse.

Within seconds Cameron Vogel, unable to assimilate what had just transpired, donned his parasail for flight. Still somewhat muddled and panic stricken he took several running steps and hurled his body into the wind. Though totally screened from his enemies by the thickening fog, in his confusion the Coventry Gardens serial killer was unable to determine whether he was pointed eastward toward land or caught up in some other compass direction- one that would spell certain doom. In any event the voices within, which had been temporarily quelled by Detective Sergeant Wilma Barnhart, remained deafly silent and offered Vogel no solution to his inexorable dilemma.

Months passed, but no sign of Cameron Vogel's remains were sighted anywhere, excepting for his mangled parasail that had been washed upon the shore of Lands End soon after the incident occurred. Though he was officially presumed dead, for all they had gone through, none of the core team participants (who experienced Vogel's unique mode of operandi) acknowledged to anyone that the Coventry Gardens serial killer had indeed been lost at sea. It seemed that everyone else remotely connected to the case had a varying opinion. So then, with that being said, what do you think?

SERGEANT STEEL'S EPILOUGE

Poised to catch up on his paper work, Sergeant Benjamin Steel glanced at the citation he received from Superintendent Carter for his heroic performance in the line of duty. Several months had elapsed since his first assignment nearly cost him his life. The sequence of events which transpired in Longships lighthouse on that last day, and the ensuing occurrences that followed, captivated Sergeant Steel incessantly.

A broad smile filled Ben's face upon recollecting Wilma Barnhart's tale of what Marshall Carter asked of her just before leaving the pier to have a heart-to-heart rendezvous with an insane serial killer. She had said to him, *"Sir, I doubt very much that I'm capable of deceiving Cameron Vogel by pretending to impersonate Melanie Belldonger's voice. It's been nearly twenty years since I last spoke to her. Isn't there anyone else you can ask?"*

Shrugging his shoulders he had simply responded, *"What's the harm in trying? From where I'm standing we're all going to die anyway."*

Steel's facial expression sobered considerably when his thoughts fast-forwarded to Sergeant Mahoney's recollection of what occurred at the time Ben and Marshall checked to see if Vogel had indeed vacated the lighthouse premises. While Miles and Wilma were descending the second tier steps with Matt carrying Tracey in his arms, the inhalation of the ocean's salt water fragrance appeared to have neutralized the pungent smell of decaying flesh. Even the bodies were mercifully shrouded by a din of darkness.

As the cutter made its way back to the mainland, and Tracey was being attended to by a bevy of medics, Steel recalled saying to Matt,

"How is it that God could possibly have allowed such a sick mind, such as Cameron Vogel's for what he's done here, to abominate His Creation?"

"God had nothing to do with it." He remembered Matt's precise reply.

"Then who did?" Ben wanted to know.

Staring into the fog, Ames had said, *"Ask the bad angel, but I doubt very much that he'll give you a straight answer."*

Sergeant Wilma Barnhart, for her gallantry under extreme pressure, had been elevated to the rank of Chief Inspector. Sergeant Mahoney's eyes exhibited tears when he received a citation of valor while being promoted to the status of Captain by Marshall Carter.

Before Matthew Ames retired from the police force, Marshall exalted him to the position of Superintendent of Scotland Yard for one day. The gesture increased his pension considerably.

Ms. Hamilton had been extraordinary resilient to the gross mental stress she'd been subjected to. Perhaps it was Tracey's marriage to Matthew Ames that heartened her to generate a spark to get on with life without having to spend serious time in rehab. As it were, in coming to grips with her grandmother's unfinished poem, Tracey decided to "let sleeping dogs lie" lest she became fixated on rekindling that part of her past which needed forever to be put to rest.

The citizens of Coventry Gardens established a memorial for all the victims who died at the hands of Cameron Vogel. Sheriff Rupert Hayes and Shire Reed Latham, because their deaths were considered an unfortunate accident not attributed to the serial killer, had not been formally eulogized in connection with the slayings. Melanie Belldonger's diary described in detail the trio's scandalous enactment pertaining to the Coventry Gardens lottery debacle. It was the first of two major issues that needed to be explained by Scotland Yard to the community in how they'd been victimized by deceit.

It had been officially recorded that a large sum of money matching the approximate figure Melanie Belldonger had etched in her memoirs, was recovered in the Penzance Hotel where Cameron Vogel had been a patron under the guise of Brandt Moore. Since the revenue rightfully belonged to the Coventry Gardens Township, it was used to give the murdered victims (including Melanie Belldonger) a proper burial- in accordance to the wishes expressed in last wills and testaments, or by surviving relatives. [Jessica O'Brien's remains (an identifiable cross had been found around the neck of her corpse) were shipped to Essex and interred next to her husband.] The remaining proceeds were used to refurbish Longships lighthouse and to defray expenses for an affordable local Cornwall emergency helicopter.

The second item of importance on the townhouse agenda referenced Cameron Vogel's clandestine movements and his use of various aliases. Parson Nathaniel Wingate's was prominent among them. Carter outlined, to the concerned citizens attending the meeting, the precise connection the serial killer and Belldonger had been caught up in- as stated in her diary. It was only fitting that the Coventry Gardens community be informed of the sordid details before what had actually happened there blanketed the media stations all over the world. Under the circumstances it was the least Scotland Yard could have done, so Marshall Carter truly believed.

Sergeant Steel realized he needed to stop reminiscing and get back to work. However, before doing so, the proud detective took up the book he had recently received from his former partner. Upon opening Agatha Christine's *Ten Little Indians* epic novel, Ben reread Matt's brief sentiments.

Greetings, Ben,

"Tracey and I are anxiously awaiting your arrival. We're delighted you accepted our invitation to spend Christmas with us. Your ticket is enclosed. Think nothing of it, partner. In case you have any doubts, to us you will always be worth your weight in gold. Give Carter and the gang a

hearty cheerio from both of us. Auckland is too good to be true. Watch your back, Mate!

All our love,
Matt and Tracey

It was then Ben's intercom beeped. "Sergeant Steel speaking," he said while replacing the Christie novel in its cradle.

The voice belonged to Carter. "I was just wondering, Sergeant Benjamin Steel, are you available to probe a triple homicide in progress? Inspector Barnhart has the case and requested that you be on her investigative team. You'll need to move your ass on this one, ex-constable. Christmas will be here before you know it." Click.

AUTHOR'S NOTE

Much of whom we are and what we've become has already been determined by how we have lived our lives; however, no one's destiny has yet been carved in stone. Whatever uncertainty may still remain in regard to anyone's wonderment of his or her eternal future, the Author of Life has sent His only Begotten Son to assist us to discover our heavenly Father.

It behooves us to take stock of what it means to love God with one's whole heart, with one's whole soul, mind, and strength- and what it entails to love one's neighbor, as we love ourselves. By integrating Jesus Christ's two great commandments of love into our daily lives, there should be no quandary in discerning that it is the sinner who must always be loved and that it is the trespasser's sin that can never be compromised.

This treatise has little to do with the fictitious likes of Cameron Vogel; but it does have everything to do with you and me. What will our final epitaphs say about us? No, not the ones reflecting mere sentiments of closure engraved on granite stone. I'm simply referencing the inevitable. Where will we stand in the end? Will we have chosen to cling to all the empty promises the good earth has promised us?

Let us not be caught up in self, or continue to intermingle with the controlling forces of those who can only promise us a delusional concept of happiness. Rather, let us be counted among those who resolutely trust in the Word of God, that what He promised to those who have humbled themselves before His Father and kept His commandments of love- will never find cause to succumb to fear. Since there's nothing of value that can replace the Holy Spirit in us, we should be ever mindful to boldly step up and claim our rightful heritages, as He has claimed each of us to be one with Him- even before the onset of His creation.

www.ingramcontent.com/pod-product-compliance
Lightning Source LLC
Chambersburg PA
CBHW032035180726
48284CB00008B/2592